THE STORY OF
BESSIE COSTRELL

THE STORY OF BESSIE COSTRELL

MRS. HUMPHRY WARD

ISBN: 978-93-90314-36-2

Published: 1912

LECTOR HOUSE LLP
E-MAIL: lectorpublishing@gmail.com

THE STORY OF
BESSIE COSTRELL

BY

MRS. HUMPHRY WARD

AUTHOR OF "ROBERT ELSMERE," "THE HISTORY OF DAVID GRIEVE,"
"MARCELLA," ETC.

1912

CONTENTS

SCENE I

It was an August evening, still and cloudy after a day unusually chilly for the time of year. Now, about sunset, the temperature was warmer than it had been in the morning, and the departing sun was forcing its way through the clouds, breaking up their level masses into delicate lattice-work of golds and greys. The last radiant light was on the wheat-fields under the hill, and on the long chalk hill itself. Against that glowing background lay the village, already engulfed by the advancing shadow. All the nearer trees, which the daylight had mingled in one green monotony, stood out sharp and distinct, each in its own plane, against the hill. Each natural object seemed to gain a new accent, a more individual beauty, from the vanishing and yet lingering sunlight.

An elderly labourer was walking along the road which led to the village. To his right lay the allotment gardens just beginning to be alive with figures, and the voices of men and children. Beyond them, far ahead, rose the square tower of the church; to his left was the hill, and straight in front of him the village, with its veils of smoke lightly brushed over the trees, and its lines of cottages climbing the chalk steeps behind it. His eye as he walked took in a number of such facts as life had trained it to notice. Once he stopped to bend over a fence, to pluck a stalk or two of oats. He examined them carefully; then he threw back his head and sniffed the air, looking all round the sky meanwhile. Yes, the season had been late and harsh, but the fine weather was coming at last. Two or three days' warmth now would ripen even the oats, let alone the wheat.

Well, he was glad. He wanted the harvest over. It would, perhaps, be his last harvest at Clinton Magna, where he had worked, man and boy, for fifty-six years come Michaelmas. His last harvest! A curious pleasure stirred the man's veins as he thought of it, a pleasure in expected change, which seemed to bring back the pulse of youth, to loosen a little the yoke at those iron years that had perforce aged and bent him; though, for sixty-two, he was still hale and strong.

Things had all come together. Here was "Muster" Hill, the farmer he had worked for these seventeen years, dying of a sudden, with a carbuncle on the neck, and the farm to be given up at Michaelmas. He—John Bolderfield—had been working on for the widow; but, in his opinion, she was "nobbut a caselty sort of body," and the sooner she and her children were taken off to Barnet, where they were to live with her mother, the less she'd cost them as had the looking after her. As for the crops, they wouldn't pay the debts; not they. And there was no one after the farm—"nary one"—and didn't seem like to be. That would make another farm on Muster Forrest's hands. Well, and a good job. Landlords must be "took down";

and there was plenty of work going on the railway just now for those that were turned off.

He was too old for the railway, though, and he might have found it hard to get fresh work if he had been staying at Clinton. But he was not staying. Poor Eliza wouldn't last more than a few days; a week or two at most, and he was not going to keep on the cottage after he'd buried her.

Aye, poor Eliza! She was his sister-in-law, the widow of his second brother. He had been his brother's lodger during the greater part of his working life, and since Tom's death he had stayed on with Eliza. She and he suited each other, and the "worritin' childer" had all gone away years since and left them in peace. He didn't believe Eliza knew where any of them were, except Mary, "married over to Luton"—and Jim and Jim's Louisa. And a good riddance too. There was not one of them knew how to keep a shilling when they'd got one. Still, it was a bit lonesome for Eliza now, with no one but Jim's Louisa to look after her.

He grew rather downhearted as he trudged along, thinking. She and he had stuck together "a many year." There would be nobody left for him to go along with when she was gone. There was his niece Bessie Costrell and her husband, and there was his silly old cousin Widow Waller. He dared say they'd both of them want him to live with them. At the thought a grin crossed his ruddy face. They both knew about *it*—that was what it was. And he wouldn't live with either of them, not he. Not yet a bit, anyway. All the same, he had a fondness for Bessie and her husband. Bessie was always very civil to *him*—he chuckled again—and if anything had to be done with it, while he was five miles off at Frampton on a job of work that had been offered him, he didn't know but he'd as soon trust Isaac Costrell and Bessie as anybody else. You might call Isaac rather a fool, what with his religion, and "extemp'ry prayin', an' that," but all the same Bolderfield thought of him with a kind of uneasy awe. If ever there was a man secure of the next world it was Isaac Costrell. His temper, perhaps, was "nassty," which might pull him down a little when the last account came to be made up; and it could not be said that his elder children had come to much, for all his piety. But, on the whole, Bolderfield only wished he stood as well with the Powers talked about in chapel every Sunday as Isaac did.

As for Bessie, she had been a wasteful woman all her life, with never a bit of money put by, and never a good dress to her back. But, "Lor' bless yer, there was a many worse folk nor Bessie." She wasn't one of your sour people—she could make you laugh; she had a merry heart. Many a pleasant evening had he passed chatting with her and Isaac; and whenever they cooked anything good there was always a bite for him. Yes, Bessie had been a good niece to him; and if he trusted any one he dared say he'd trust them.

"Well, how's Eliza, Muster Bolderfield?" said a woman who passed him in the village street.

He replied, and then went on his way, sobered again, dreading to find himself at the cottage once more, and in the stuffy upper room with the bed and the dying woman. Yet he was not really sad, not here at least, out in the air and the sun.

There was always a thought in his mind, a fact in his consciousness, which stood between him and sadness. It had so stood for a long, long time. He walked through the village to-night, in spite of Eliza and his sixty years, with a free bearing and a confident glance to right and left. He knew, and the village knew, that he was not as other men.

He passed the village green with its pond, and began to climb a lane leading to the hill. Half-way up stood two cottages sideways. Phloxes and marigolds grew untidily about their doorways, and straggly roses, starved a little by the chalk soil, looked in at their latticed windows. They were, however, comparatively modern and comfortable, with two bedrooms above and two living-rooms below, far superior to the older and more picturesque cottages in the main street.

John went in softly, put down his straw dinner-bag, and took off his heavy boots. Then he opened a door in the wall of the kitchen, and gently climbed the stairs.

A girl was sitting by the bed. When she saw his whitish head and red face emerge against the darkness of the stair-hole, she put up her finger for silence.

John crept in and came to look at the patient. His eyes grew round and staring, his colour changed.

"Is she a-goin'?" he said, with evident excitement.

Jim's Louisa shook her head. She was rather a stupid girl, heavy and round-faced, but she had nursed her grandmother well.

"No; she's asleep. Muster Drew's been here, and she dropped off while he was a-talkin' to her."

Mr. Drew was the Congregational minister.

"Did she send for him?"

"Yes; she said she felt her feet a-gettin' cold, and I must run. But I don't believe she's no worse."

John stood looking down, ruefully. Suddenly the figure in the bed turned.

"John," said a comparatively strong voice which made Bolderfield start— "John, Muster Drew says you'd oughter put it in the bank. You'll be a fool if yer don't, 'ee says."

The old woman's pinched face emerged from the sheets, looking up at him. Bluish patches showed here and there on the drawn white skin; there was a great change since the morning, but the eyes were still alive.

John was silent a moment, one corner of his mouth twitching, as though what she had said struck him in a humorous light.

"Well, I don't know as I mind much what 'ee says, 'Liza."

"Sit down."

She made a movement with her emaciated hand. John sat down on the chair Louisa gave up to him, and bent down over the bed.

"If yer woan't do—what Muster Drew says, John—whatever *wull* yer do with it?"

She spoke slowly, but clearly. John scratched his head. His complexion had evidently been very fair. It was still fresh and pink, and the full cheek hung a little over the jaw. The mouth was shrewd, but its expression was oddly contradicted by the eyes, which had on the whole a childish, weak look.

"I think yer must leave it to me, 'Liza," he said at last. "I'll do all for the best."

"No—yer'll not, John," said the dying voice. "You'd a done a many stupid things—if I 'adn't stopped yer. An' I'm a-goin'. You'll never leave it wi' Bessie?"

"An' who 'ud yer 'ave me leave it with? Ain't Bessie my own sister's child?"

An emaciated hand stole out of the bed-clothes and fastened feebly on his arm.

"If yer do, John, yer'll repent it. Yer never were a good one at judgin' folk. Yer doan't consider nothin'—an' I'm a-goin'. Leave it with Saunders, John."

There was a pause. Then John said with an obstinate look—

"Saunders 'as never been a friend o' mine since 'ee did me out o' that bit o' business with Missus Moulsey. An' I don't mean to go makin' friends with him again."

Eliza withdrew her hand with a long sigh, and her eyelids closed. A fit of coughing shook her; she had to be lifted in bed, and it left her gasping and death-ly. John was sorely troubled, and not only for himself. When she was more at ease again, he stooped to her and put his mouth to her ear.

"'Liza, don't yer think no more about it. Did Mr. Drew read to yer? Are yer comfortable in yer mind?"

She made a sign of assent, which showed, however, no great interest in the subject. There was silence for a long time. Louisa was getting supper downstairs. John, oppressed by the heat of the room and tired by his day's work, had almost fallen asleep in his chair, when the old woman spoke again.

"John—what 'ud you think o' Mary Anne Waller?"

The whisper was still human and eager.

John roused himself, and could not help an astonished laugh.

"Why, whatever put Mary Anne into your head, 'Liza? Yer never thought any-think o' Mary Anne—no more than me."

Eliza's eyes wandered round the room.

"P'r'aps——" she said, then stopped, and could say no more. She seemed to become unconscious, and John went to call for Louisa.

In the middle of the night John woke with a start, and sat up to listen. Not a sound—but they would have called him if the end had come. He could not rest, however, and presently he huddled on some clothes and went to listen at Eliza's door. It was ajar, and, hearing nothing, he pushed it open.

Poor Eliza lay in her agony, unconscious, and breathing heavily. Beside her sat the widow, Mary Anne Waller, and Louisa, motionless too, their heads bent. There was an end of candle in a basin behind the bed, which threw circles of wavering light over the coarse whitewash of the roof and on the cards and faded photographs above the tiny mantelpiece.

John crept up to the bed. The two women made a slight movement to let him stand between them.

"Can't yer give her no brandy?" he asked, whispering.

Mary Anne Waller shook her head.

"Dr. Murch said we wer'n't to trouble her. She'll go when the light comes—most like."

She was a little shrivelled woman with a singularly delicate mouth, that quivered as she spoke. John and Eliza Bolderfield had never thought much of her, though she was John's cousin. She was a widow, and greatly "put upon" both by her children and her neighbours. Her children were grown up, and settled—more or less—in the world, but they still lived on her freely whenever it suited them; and in the village generally she was reckoned but a poor creature.

However, when Eliza—originally a hard, strong woman—took to her bed with incurable disease, Mary Anne Waller came in to help, and was accepted. She did everything humbly; she even let Louisa order her about. But before the end, Eliza had come to be restless when she was not there.

Now, however, Eliza knew no more, and the little widow sat gazing at her with the tears on her cheeks. John, too, felt his eyes wet.

But after half an hour, when there was still no change, he was turning away to go back to bed, when the widow touched his arm.

"Won't yer give her a kiss, John?" she said timidly. "She wor a good sister to you."

John, with a tremor, stooped, and clumsily did as he was told—the first time in his life he had ever done so for Mary Anne. Then, stepping as noiselessly as he could on his bare feet, he hurried away. A man shares nothing of that yearning attraction which draws women to a death-bed as such. Instead, John felt a sudden sickness at his heart. He was thankful to find himself in his own room again, and thought with dread of having to go back—for the end. In spite of his still vigorous and stalwart body, he was often plagued with nervous fears and fancies. And it was years now since he had seen death—he had, indeed, carefully avoided seeing it.

Gradually, however, as he sat on the edge of his bed in the summer dark, the new impression died away, and something habitual took its place—that shielding, solacing thought, which was in truth all the world to him, and was going to make up to him for Eliza's death, for getting old, and the lonesomeness of a man without chick or child. He would have felt unutterably forlorn and miserable, he would have shrunk trembling from the shapes of death and pain that seemed to fill the darkness, but for this fact, this defence, this treasure, that set him apart from his fellows and gave him this proud sense of superiority, of a good time coming in spite of all. Instinctively, as he sat on the bed, he pushed his bare foot backwards till his heel touched a wooden object that stood underneath. The contact cheered him at once. He ceased to think about Eliza, his head was once more full of whirling plans and schemes.

The wooden object was a box that held his money, the savings of a labourer's lifetime. Seventy-one pounds! It seemed to him an ocean of gold, never to be exhausted. The long toil of saving it was almost done. After the Frampton job, he would begin enjoying it, cautiously at first, taking a bit of work now and again, and then a bit of holiday.

All the savour of life was connected for him with that box. His mind ran over the constant excitements of the many small loans he had made from it to his relations and friends. A shilling in the pound interest—he had never taken less and he had never asked more. He had only lent to people he knew well, people in the village whom he could look after, and seldom for a term longer than three months, for to be parted from his money at all gave him physical pain. He had once suffered great anxiety over a loan to his eldest brother of thirty pounds. But in the end James had paid it all back. He could still feel tingling through him the passionate joy with which he had counted out the recovered sovereigns, with the extra three half-sovereigns of interest.

Muster Drew indeed! John fell into an angry inward argument against his suggestion of the savings bank. It was an argument he had often rehearsed, often declaimed, and at bottom it all came to this—without that box under his bed, his life would have sunk to dulness and decrepitude; he would have been merely a pitiful and lonely old man. He had neither wife nor children, all for the hoard's sake; but while the hoard was there, to be handled any hour, he regretted nothing. Besides, there was the peasant's rooted distrust of offices, and paper transactions, of any routine that checks his free will and frightens his inexperience. He was still eagerly thinking when the light began to flood into his room, and before he could compose himself to sleep the women called him.

But he shed no more tears. He saw Eliza die, his companion of forty years, and hardly felt it. What troubled him all through the last scene was the thought that now he should never know why she was so set against "Bessie's 'avin' it."

SCENE II

It was, indeed, the general opinion in Clinton Magna that John Bolderfield—or "Borrofull," as the village pronounced it, took his sister-in-law's death too lightly. The women especially pronounced him a hard heart. Here was "poor Eliza" gone, Eliza who had kept him decent and comfortable for forty years, ever since he was a lad, and he could go about whistling, and—to talk to him—as gay as a lark! Yet John contributed handsomely to the burial expenses—Eliza having already, through her burial club, provided herself with a more than regulation interment; and he gave Jim's Louisa her mourning. Nevertheless, these things did not avail. It was felt instinctively that he was not beaten down as he ought to have been, and Mrs. Saunders, the smith's wife, was applauded when she said to her neighbours that "you couldn't expeck a man with John Bolderfield's money to have as many feelin's as other people." Whence it would seem that the capitalist is no more truly popular in small societies than in large.

John, however, did not trouble himself about these things. He was hard at work harvesting for Muster Hill's widow, and puzzling his head day and night as to what to do with his box.

When the last field had been carried and the harvest supper was over, he came home late, and wearied out. His working life at Clinton Magna was done; and the family he had worked for so long was broken up in distress and poverty. Yet he felt only a secret exultation. Such toil and effort behind—such a dreamland in front!

Next day he set to work to wind up his affairs. The furniture of the cottage was left to Eliza's son Jim, and the daughter had arranged for the carting of it to the house twelve miles off where her parents lived. She was to go with it on the morrow, and John would give up the cottage and walk over to Frampton, where he had already secured a lodging.

Only twenty-four hours!—and he had not yet decided. Which was it to be—Saunders, after all—or the savings bank—or Bessie?

He was cording up his various possessions—a medley lot—in different parcels and bundles when Bessie Costrell knocked at the door. She had already offered to stow away anything he might like to leave with her.

"Well, I thought you'd be busy," she said as she walked in, "an' I came up to lend a hand. Is them the things you're goin' to leave me to take care on?"

John nodded.

"Field's cart, as takes Louisa's things to-morrer, is a-goin' to deliver these at your place first. They're more nor I thought they would be. But you can put 'em anywheres."

"Oh, I'll see to them."

She sat down and watched him tie the knots of the last parcel.

"There's some people as is real ill-natured," she said presently, in an angry voice.

"Aye?" said John, looking up sharply. "What are they sayin' now?"

"It's Muster Saunders. 'Ee's allus sayin' nassty things about other folks. And there'd be plenty of fault to be found with 'im, if onybody was to try. An' Sally Saunders eggs him on dreadful."

Saunders was the village smith, a tall, brawny man, of great size and corresponding wisdom, who had been the village arbiter and general councillor for a generation. There was not a will made in Clinton Magna that he did not advise upon; not a bit of contentious business that he had not a share in; not a family history that he did not know. His probity was undisputed; his ability was regarded with awe; but as he had a sharp tongue and was no respecter of persons, there was of course an opposition.

John took a seat on the wooden box he had just been cording, and mopped his brow. His full cheeks were crimson, partly with exertion, partly with sudden annoyance.

"What's 'ee been sayin' now? Though it doan't matter a brass farthin' to me what 'ee says."

"He says you 'aven't got no proper feelin's about poor Eliza, an' you'd ought to have done a great deal more for Louisa. But 'ee says you allus were a mean one with your money—an' you knew that '*ee* knew it—for 'ee'd stopped you takin' an unfair advantage more nor once. An' 'ee didn't believe as your money would come to any good; for now Eliza was gone you wouldn't know how to take care on it."

John's eyes flamed.

"Oh! 'ee says that, do 'ee? Well, Saunders wor allus a beast—an' a beast 'ee'll be."

He sat with his chin on his large dirty hands, ruminating furiously.

It was quite true that Saunders had thwarted him more than once. There was old Mrs. Moulsey at the shop, when she wanted to buy those cottages in Potter's Row—and there was Sam Field the higgler—both of them would have borrowed from him if Saunders hadn't cooled them off. Saunders said it was a Jew's interest he was asking—because there was security—but he wasn't going to accept a farthing less than his shilling a pound for three months—not he! So they might take it or leave it. And Mrs. Moulsey got hers from the Building Society, and Sam Field made shift to go without. And John Bolderfield was three pounds poorer that quarter than he need have been—all along of Saunders. And now Saunders was talking "agen him" like this—blast him!

"Oh, an' then he went on," pursued Bessie with gusto, "about your bein' too ignorant to put it in the post-office. 'Ee said you'd think Edwards would go an' spend it" (Edwards was the post-master), "an' then he laughed fit to split 'imself. Yer couldn't see more nor the length of your own nose, he said — it was edication *you* wanted. As for 'im, 'ee said, 'ee'd have kep' it for you if you'd asked him, but you'd been like a bear with a sore 'ead, 'ee said, ever since Mrs. Moulsey's affair — so 'ee didn't suppose you would."

"Well, 'ee's about right there," said John, grimly; "ee's talkin' sense for onst when 'ee says that. I'd dig a hole in the hill and bury it sooner nor I'd trust it to 'im — I would, by — —" he swore vigorously. "A thieving set of magpies is all them Saunders — cadgin' 'ere and cadgin' there."

He spoke with fierce contempt, the tacit hatred of years leaping to sight. Bessie's bright brown eyes looked at him with sympathy.

"It was just his nassty spite," she said. "He knew *'ee* could never ha' done it — not what you've done — out o' your wages. Not unless 'ee got Sally to tie 'im to the dresser with ropes so as 'ee couldn't go a-near the Spotted Deer no more!"

She laughed like a merry child at her own witticism, and John relished it too, though he was not in a laughing mood.

"Why," continued Bessie with enthusiasm, "it was Muster Drew as said to me the other afternoon, as we was walkin' 'ome from the churchyard, says 'ee, 'Mrs. Costrell, I call it splendid what John's done — I *do*,' 'ee says. 'A labourer on fifteen shillin's a week — why, it's an example to the county,' 'ee says. ''Ee ought to be showed.'"

John's face relaxed. The temper and obstinacy in the eyes began to yield to the weak complacency which was their more normal expression.

There was silence for a minute or two. Bessie sat with her hands on her lap and her face turned towards the open door. Beyond the cherry-red phloxes outside it the ground fell rapidly to the village, rising again beyond the houses to a great stubble field, newly shorn. Gleaners were already in the field, their bent figures casting sharp shadows on the golden upland, and the field itself stretched upwards to a great wood that lay folded round the top of a spreading hill. To the left, beyond the hill, a wide plain travelled into the sunset, its level spaces cut by the scrawled elms and hedgerows of the nearer landscape. The beauty of it all — the beauty of an English midland — was of a modest and measured sort, depending chiefly on bounties of sun and air, on the delicacies of gentle curves and the pleasant intermingling of wood and cornfield, of light spaces with dark, of solid earth and luminous sky.

Such as it was, however, neither Bessie nor John spared it a moment's attention. Bessie was thinking a hundred busy thoughts. John, on the other hand, had begun to consider her with an excited scrutiny. She was a handsome woman, as she sat in the doorway with her fine brown head turned to the light. But John naturally was not thinking of that. He was in the throes of decision.

"Look 'ere, Bessie," he said suddenly; "what 'ud you say if I wor to ask Isaac an' you to take care on it?"

Bessie started slightly. Then she looked frankly round at him. She had very keen, lively eyes, and a bright red-brown colour on thin cheeks. The village applied to her the epithet which John's thoughts had applied to Muster Hill's widow. They said she was "caselty," which means flighty, haphazard, excitable; but she was popular, nevertheless, and had many friends.

It was, of course, her own settled opinion that her uncle ought to leave that box with her and Isaac; and it had wounded her vanity, and her affection besides, that John had never yet made any such proposal, though she knew—as, indeed, the village knew—that he was perplexed as to what to do with his hoard. But she had never dared to suggest that he should leave it with her, out of fear of Eliza Bolderfield. Bessie was well aware that Eliza thought ill of her, and would dissuade John from any such arrangement if she could. And so formidable was Eliza—a woman of the hardest and sourest virtue—when she chose, that Bessie was afraid of her, even on her deathbed, though generally ready enough to quarrel with other people. Nevertheless, Bessie had always felt that it would be a crying shame and slight if she and Isaac did not have the guardianship of the money. She thirsted, perhaps, to make an impression upon public opinion in the village, which, as she instinctively realised, held her cheaply. And then, of course, there was the secret thought of John's death, and what might come of it. John had always loudly proclaimed that he meant to spend his money, and not leave it behind him. But the instinct of saving, once formed, is strong. John, too, might die sooner than he thought—and she and Isaac had children.

She had come up, indeed, that afternoon, haunted by a passionate desire to get the money into her hands; yet the mere sordidness of "expectations" counted for less in the matter than one would suppose. Vanity, a vague wish to ingratiate herself with her uncle, to avoid a slight—these were, on the whole, her strongest motives. At any rate, when he had once asked her the momentous question, she knew well what to say to him.

"Well, if you arst me," she said hastily, "of course *we* think as it's only nateral you should leave it with Isaac an' me, as is your own kith and kin. But we wasn't goin' to say nothin'; we didn't want to be pushin' of ourselves forward."

John rose to his feet. He was in his shirt-sleeves, which were rolled up. He pulled them down, put on his coat, an air of crisis on his fat face.

"Where 'ud you put it?" he said.

"Yer know that cupboard by the top of the stairs? It 'ud stand there easy. And the cupboard's got a good lock to it; but we'd 'ave it seen to, to make sure."

She looked up at him eagerly. She longed to feel herself trusted and important. Her self-love was too often mortified in these respects.

John fumbled round his neck for the bit of black cord on which he kept two keys—the key of his room while he was away and the key of the box itself.

"Well, let's get done with it," he said. "I'm off to-morrer mornin', six o'clock. You go and get Isaac to come down."

"I'll run," said Bessie, catching up her shawl and throwing it over her head. "He wor just finishin' his tea."

And she whirled out of the cottage, running up the steep road behind it as fast as she could. John was vaguely displeased by her excitement; but the die was cast. He went to make his arrangements.

Bessie ran till she was out of breath. When she reached her own house, a cottage in a side lane above the Bolderfields' cottage and overlooking it from the back, she found her husband sitting with his pipe at the open door and reading his newspaper. Three out of her own four children were playing in the lane, otherwise there was no one about.

Isaac greeted her with a nod and slight lightening of the eyes, which, however, hardly disturbed the habitual sombreness of the face. He was a dark, finely featured man, with grizzled hair, carrying himself with an air of sleepy melancholy. He was much older than his wife, and was a prominent leader in the little Independent chapel of the village. His melancholy could give way on occasion to fits of violent temper. For instance, he had been almost beside himself when Bessie, who had leanings to the Establishment, as providing a far more crowded and entertaining place of resort on Sundays than her husband's chapel, had rashly proposed to have the youngest baby christened in church. Other Independents did it freely—why not she? But Isaac had been nearly mad with wrath, and Bessie had fled upstairs from him, with her baby, and bolted the bedroom door in bodily terror. Otherwise, he was a most docile husband—in the neighbours' opinion, docile to absurdity. He complained of nothing, and took notice of little. Bessie's untidy ways left him indifferent; his main interest was in a kind of religious dreaming, and in an Independent paper to which he occasionally wrote a letter. He was a gardener at a small house on the hill, and had rather more education than most of his fellows in the village. For the rest, he was fond of his children, and, in his heart of hearts, exceedingly proud of his wife, her liveliness and her good looks. She had been a remarkably pretty girl when he married her, some eight years after his first wife's death, and there was a great difference of age between them. His two elder children by his first marriage had long since left home. The girl was in service. It troubled him to think of the boy, who had fallen into bad ways early. Bessie's children were all small, and she herself still young, though over thirty.

When Bessie came up to him, she looked round to see that no one could hear. Then she stooped and told him her errand in a panting whisper. He must go down and fetch the box at once. She had promised John Borrofull that they would stand by him. They were his own flesh and blood—and the cupboard had a capital lock—and there wasn't no fear of it at all.

Isaac listened to her at first with amazement, then sulkily. She had talked to him often certainly about John's money, but it had made little impression on his dreamer's sense. And now her demand struck him disagreeably.

He didn't want the worrit of other people's money, he said. Let them as owned it keep it; filthy lucre was a snare to all as had to do with it; and it would only bring a mischief to have it in the house.

After a few more of these objections, Bessie lost her temper. She broke into a torrent of angry arguments and reproaches, mainly turning, it seemed, upon a recent visit to the house of Isaac's eldest son. The drunken ne'er-do-weel had given Bessie much to put up with. Oh yes!—*she* was to be plagued out of her life by Isaac's belongings, and he wouldn't do a pin's worth for her. Just let him see next time, that was all.

Isaac smoked vigorously through it all. But she was hammering on a sore point.

"Oh, it's just like yer!" Bessie flung at him at last in desperation. "You're allus the same—a mean-spirited feller, stannin' in your children's way! 'Ow do *you* know who old John's going to leave his money to? 'Ow do *you* know as he wouldn't leave it to *them* poor innercents"—she waved her hand tragically towards the children playing in the road—"if we was just a bit nice and friendly with him now 'ee's gettin' old? But you don't care, not you!—one 'ud think yer were made o' money—an' that little un there not got the right use of his legs!"

She pointed, half crying, to the second boy, who had already shown signs of hip disease.

Isaac still smoked, but he was troubled in his mind. A vague presentiment held him, but the pressure brought to bear upon him was strong.

"I tell yer the lock isn't a good 'un!" he said, suddenly removing his pipe.

Bessie stopped instantly in the middle of another tirade. She was leaning against the door, arms akimbo, eyes alternately wet and flaming.

"Then, if it isn't," she said, with a triumphant change of tone, "I'll soon get Flack to see to it—it's nobbut a step. I'll run up after supper."

Flack was the village carpenter.

"An' there's mother's old box as takes up the cupboard," continued Isaac gruffly.

Bessie burst out laughing.

"Oh! yer old silly," she said. "As if they couldn't stand one top o' the t'other. Now, do just go, Isaac—there's a lovey! 'Ee's waitin' for yer. Whatever did make yer so contrairy? Of course I didn't mean nothin' I said—an' I don't mind Timothy, nor nothin'."

Still he did not move.

"Then I s'pose yer want everybody in the village to know?" he said with sarcasm.

Bessie was taken aback.

"No—I—don't—" she said undecidedly—"I don't know what yer mean."

"You go back and tell John as I'll come when it's dark, an', if he's not a stupid, he won't want me to come afore."

Bessie understood and acquiesced. She ran back with her message to John.

At half-past eight, when it had grown almost dark, Isaac descended the hill. John opened the door to his knock.

"Good evenin', Isaac. Yer'll take it, will yer?"

"If you can't do nothin' better with it," said Isaac, unwillingly. "But in gineral I'm not partial on keeping other folk's money."

John liked him all the better for his reluctance.

"It'll give yer no trouble," he said. "You lock it up, an' it'll be all safe. Now, will yer lend a hand?"

Isaac stepped to the door, looked up the lane, and saw that all was quiet. Then he came back, and the two men raised the box.

As they crossed the threshold, however, the door of the next cottage—which belonged to Watson, the policeman—opened suddenly. John, in his excitement, was so startled that he almost dropped his end of the box.

"Why, Bolderfield," said Watson's cheery voice, "what have you got there? Do you want a hand?"

"No, I don't—thank yer kindly," said John in agitation. "An', if *you* please, Muster Watson, don't yer say nothin' to nobody."

The burly policeman looked from John to Isaac, then at the box. John's hoard was notorious, and the officer of the law understood.

"Lor' bless yer," he said, with a laugh, "I'm safe. Well, good evenin' to yer, if I can't be of any assistance."

And he went off on his beat.

The two men carried the box up the hill. It was in itself a heavy, old-fashioned affair, strengthened and bottomed with iron. Isaac wondered whether the weight of it were due more to the box or to the money. But he said nothing. He had no idea how much John might have saved, and would not have asked him the direct question for the world. John's own way of talking about his wealth was curiously contradictory. His "money" was rarely out of his thoughts or speech, but no one had ever been privileged for many years now to see the inside of his box, except Eliza once; and no one but himself knew the exact amount of the hoard. It delighted him that the village gossips should double or treble it. Their estimates only gave him the more ground for vague boasting, and he would not have said a word to put them right.

When they reached the Costrells' cottage, John's first care was to examine the cupboard. He saw that the large wooden chest filled with odds and ends of rubbish which already stood there was placed on the top of his own box. Then he tried the lock, and pronounced it adequate; he didn't want to have Flack meddling round. Now, at the moment of parting with his treasure, he was seized with a sudden fever of secrecy. Bessie meanwhile hovered about the two men, full of excitement and loquacity. And the children, shut into the kitchen, wondered what could be the matter.

When all was done, Isaac locked the cupboard, and solemnly presented the key to John, who added it to the other round his neck. Then Bessie unlocked the kitchen, and sent the children flying, to help her with the supper. She was in her most bustling and vivacious mood, and she had never cooked the bloaters better or provided a more ample jug of beer. But John was silent and depressed.

He took leave at last with many sighs and lingerings. But he had not been gone half an hour, and Bessie and Isaac were just going to bed, when there was a knock at the door, and he reappeared.

"Let me lie down there," he said, pointing to a broken-down old sofa that ran under the window. "I'm lonesome somehow, an' I've told Louisa." His white hair and whiskers stood out wildly round his red face. He looked old and ill, and the sympathetic Bessie was sorry for him.

She made him a bed on the sofa, and he lay there all night, restless, and sighing heavily. He missed Eliza more than he had done yet, and was oppressed with a vague sense of unhappiness. Once, in the middle of the night when all was still, he stole upstairs in his stockinged feet and gently tried the cupboard door. It was quite safe, and he went down contented.

An hour or two later he was off, trudging to Frampton through the August dawn, with his bundle on his back.

SCENE III

Some five months passed away.

One January night the Independent minister of Clinton Magna was passing down the village street. Clinton lay robed in light snow, and "sparkling to the moon." The frozen pond beside the green, though it was nearly eight o'clock, was still alive with children, sliding and shouting. All around the gabled roofs stood laden and spotless. The woods behind the village, and those running along the top of the snowy hill, were meshed in a silvery mist which died into the moonlit blue, while in the fields the sharpness of the shadows thrown by the scattered trees made a marvel of black and white.

The minister, in spite of a fighting creed, possessed a measure of gentler susceptibilities, and the beauty of this basin in the chalk hills, this winter triumphant, these lights of home and fellowship in the cottage windows disputing the forlornness of the snow, crept into his soul. His mind travelled from the physical purity and hardness before him to the purity and hardness of the inner life—the purity that Christ blessed, the "hardness" that the Christian endures. And such thoughts brought him pleasure as he walked—the mystic's pleasure.

Suddenly he saw a woman cross the snowy green in front of him. She had come from the road leading to the hill, and her pace was hurried. Her shawl was muffled round her head, but he recognised her, and his mood fell. She was the wife of Isaac Costrell, and she was hurrying to the Spotted Deer, a public-house which lay just beyond the village, on the road to the mill. Already several times that week had he seen her going in or coming out. Talk had begun to reach him, and he said to himself to-night as he saw her—that Isaac Costrell's wife was going to ruin.

The thought oppressed him, pricked his pastoral conscience. Isaac was his right-hand man: dull to all the rest of the world, but not dull to the minister. With Mr. Drew sometimes he would break into talk of religion, and the man's dark eyes would lose their film. His big troubled self spoke with that accent of truth which lifts common talk and halting texts to poetry. The minister, himself more of a pessimist than his sermons showed, felt a deep regard for him. Could nothing be done to save Isaac's wife and Isaac? Not so long ago Bessie Costrell had been a decent woman, though a flighty and excitable one. Now some cause, unknown to the minister, had upset a wavering balance, and was undoing a life.

As he passed the public-house a man came out, and through the open door Mr. Drew caught a momentary glimpse of the bar and the drinkers. Bessie's handsome, reckless head stood out an instant in the bright light.

Then Drew saw that the man who had emerged was Watson the policeman. They greeted each other cordially and walked on together. Watson also was a member of the minister's flock. Mr. Drew felt suddenly moved to unburden himself.

"That was Costrell's wife, Watson, wasn't it, poor thing?"

"Aye, it wor Mrs. Costrell," said Watson in the tone of concern natural to the respectable husband and father.

The minister sighed. "It's terrible the way she's gone downhill the last three months. I never pass almost but I see her going in there or coming out."

"No," said Watson, slowly, "no, it's bad. What I'd like to know," he added reflectively, "is where she gets the money from."

"Oh, she had a legacy, hadn't she, in August? It seems to have been a curse. She has been a changed woman ever since."

"Yes, she had a legacy," said Watson dubiously; "but I don't believe it was much. She talked big, of course, and made a lot o' fuss—she's that kind o' woman—just as she did about old John's money."

"Old John's money?—Ah! did any one ever know what became of that?"

"Well, there's many people thinks as Isaac has got it hid in the house somewhere, and there's others thinks he's put it in Bedford bank. Edwards told me private he didn't know nothing about it at the post-office, an' Bessie told my wife as John had given Isaac the keepin' of it till he come back again; but he'd knock her about, she said, if she let on what he'd done with it. That's the story she's allus had, and boastin', of course, dreadful, about John's trustin' them, and Isaac doin' all his business for him."

The minister reflected.—"And you say the legacy wasn't much?"

"Well, sir, I know some people over at Bedford where her aunt lived as left it her, and they were sure it wasn't a great deal; but you never know."

"And Isaac never said?"

"Bless yer, no, sir! He was never a great one for talking, wasn't Isaac; but you'd think now as he'd never learnt how. He'll set there in the Club of a night and never open his mouth to nobody."

"Perhaps he's fretting about his wife, Watson?"

"Well, I don't believe as he knows much about her goin's-on—not all, leastways. I've seen her wait till he was at his work or gone to the Club, and then run down the hill,—tearin'—with her hair flyin'—you'd think she'd gone silly. Oh, it's a bad business," said Watson, strongly, "an' uncommon bad business—all them young children too."

"I never saw her drunk, Watson."

"No—yer wouldn't. Nor I neither. But she'll treat half the parish if she gets the chance. I know many young fellers as go to the Spotted Deer just because they know she'll treat 'em, She's a-doin' of it now—there's lots of 'em. And allus changin' such a queer lot of money too—odd half-crowns—years and years old—King George the Third, sir. No—it's strange—very strange."

The two walked on into the darkness, still talking.

Meanwhile, inside the Spotted Deer Bessie Costrell was treating her hangers-on. She had drunk one glass of gin and water—it had made a beauty of her in the judgment of the tap-room, such a kindling had it given to her brown eyes and such a redness to her cheek. Bessie, in truth, had reached her moment of physical prime. The marvel was that there were no lovers in addition to the drinking and the extravagance. But the worst of the village scandal-mongers knew of none. Since this new phase of character in her had developed, she would drink and make merry with any young fellow in the place, but it went no farther. She was *bonne camarade* with all the world—no more. Perhaps at bottom some coolness of temperament protected her; nobody, at any rate, suspected that it had anything to do with Isaac, or that she cared a ha'porth for so lugubrious and hypocritical a husband.

She had showered drinks on all her friends, and had, moreover, chattered and screamed herself hoarse, when the church-clock outside slowly struck eight. She started, changed countenance, and got up to pay at once.

"Why, there's another o' them half-crowns o' yourn, Bessie," said a consumptive-looking girl in a bedraggled hat and feathers, as Mrs. Costrell handed her coin to the landlord. "Wheriver do yer get 'em?"

"If yer don't ask no questions, I won't tell yer no lies," said Bessie, with quick impudence. "Where did you get them hat and feathers?"

There was a coarse laugh from the company. The girl in the hat reddened furiously, and she and Bessie—both of them in a quarrelsome state—began to bandy words.

Meanwhile the landlord was showing the coin to his assistant at the bar.

"Rum, ain't it? I niver seed one o' them pieces in the village afore this winter, an' I've been 'ere twenty-two year come April."

A decent-looking labourer, who did not often visit the Spotted Deer, was leaning over the bar and caught the words.

"Well, then, I 'ave," he said promptly. "I mind well as when I were a lad, sixteen year ago, my fayther borrered a bit o' money off John Bolderfield, to buy a cow with—an' there was 'arf of it in them 'arf-crowns."

Those standing near overheard. Bessie and the girl stopped quarrelling. The landlord, startled, cast a sly eye in Bessie's direction. She came up to the bar.

"What's that yer sayin'?" she demanded. The man repeated his remark.

"Well, I dessay there was," said Bessie—"I dessay there was. I s'pose there's plenty of 'em. Where do I get 'em?—why, I get 'em at Bedford, of course, when I goes for my money."

She looked round defiantly. No one said anything; but everybody instinctively suspected a lie. The sudden silence was striking.

"Well, give me my change, will yer?" she said impatiently to the landlord. "I can't stan' here all night."

He gave it to her, and she went out showering reckless good-nights, to which there was little response. The door had no sooner closed upon her than every one in the tap-room pressed round the bar in a close gathering of heads and tongues.

Bessie ran across the green and began to climb the hill at a rapid pace. Her thin woollen shawl blown back by the wind left her arms and bosom exposed. But the effects of the spirit in her veins prevented any sense of cold, though it was a bitter night.

Once or twice, as she toiled up the hill, she gave a loud sudden sob.

"Oh, my God!" she said to herself. "My God!"

When she was half-way up she met a neighbour.

"Have yer seen Isaac?" Bessie asked her, panting.

"'Ee's at the Club, arn't 'ee?" said the woman. "Well, they won't be up yet. Jim tolt me as Muster Perris"—Muster Perris was the vicar of Clinton Magna—"'ad got a strange gen'leman stayin' with 'im, and was goin' to take him into the Club to-night to speak to 'em. 'Ee's a bishop, they ses—someun from furrin parts."

Bessie threw her good-night and climbed on.

When she reached the cottage the lamp was flaming on the table and the fire was bright. Her lame boy had done all she had told him, and her miserable heart softened. She hurriedly put out some food for Isaac. Then she lit a candle and went up to look at the children. They were all asleep in the room to the right of the stairs—the two little boys in one bed, the two little girls in the other, each pair huddled together against the cold, like dormice in a nest. Then she looked, conscience-stricken, at the untidiness of the room. She had bought the children a wonderful number of new clothes lately, and, the family being quite unused to such abundance, there was no place to keep them in. A new frock was flung down in a corner just as it had been taken off; the kitten was sleeping on Arthur's last new jacket; a smart hat with a bunch of poppies in it was lying about the floor; and under the iron beds could be seen a confusion of dusty boots, new and old. The children were naturally reckless, like their mother, and they had been getting used to new things. What excited them now, more than the acquisitions themselves, was that their mother had strictly forbidden them ever to show any of their new clothes to their father. If they did, she would beat them well, she said. That they understood; and life was thereby enriched, not only by new clothes but by a number of new emotions and terrors.

If Bessie noted the state of the room, she made no attempt to mend it. She smoothed back the hair from the boys' foreheads with a violent, shaky hand, and kissed them all, especially Arthur. Then she went out and closed the door behind her.

Outside she stood a moment on the tiny landing—listening. Not a sound; but the cottage walls were thin. If any one came along the lane with heavy boots she must hear them. Very like he would be half an hour yet.

She ran down the stairs and shut the door at the bottom of them, opening into the kitchen. It had no key, or she would have locked it; and in her agitation, her state of clouded brain, she forgot the outer door altogether. Hurrying up again, she sat down on the topmost step, putting her candle on the boards beside her. The cupboard at the stair-head where John had left his money was close to her left hand.

As she sank into the attitude of rest, her first instinct was to cry and bemoan herself. Deep in her woman's being great floods of tears were rising, and would fain have spent themselves. But she fought them down, rapidly passing instead into a state of cold terror—terror of Isaac's step—terror of discovery—of the man in the public-house.

There was a mousehole in the skirting of the stairs close to the cupboard. She slipped in a finger, felt along an empty space behind, and drew out a key.

It turned easily in the cupboard lock, and the two boxes stood revealed, standing apparently just as they stood when John left them. In hot haste Bessie dragged the treasure-box from under the other, starting at every sound in the process, at the thud the old wooden trunk made on the floor of the cupboard as its supporter was withdrawn, at the rustle of her own dress. All the boldness she had shown at the Spotted Deer had vanished. She was now the mere trembling and guilty woman.

The lock on Bolderfield's box had been forced long before; it opened to her hand. A heap of sovereigns and half-sovereigns lay on one side, divided by a wooden partition from the few silver coins, crowns and half-crowns, still lying on the other. She counted both the gold and silver, losing her reckoning again and again, because of the sudden anguish of listening that would overtake her.

Thirty-six pounds on the one side, not much more than thirty shillings on the other. When John left it there had been fifty-one pounds in gold, and rather more than twenty pounds in silver, most of it in half-crowns. Ah! she knew the figures well.

Did that man who had spoken to the landlord in the public-house suspect? How strange they had all looked! What a silly fool she had been to change so much of the silver, instead of sticking to the gold! Yet she had thought the gold would be noticed more.

When was old John coming back? He had written once from Frampton to say that he was "laid up bad with the rheumatics," and was probably going into the Frampton Infirmary. That was in November. Since then nothing had been heard of him. John was no scholar. What if he died without coming back? There would be no trouble then, except—except with Isaac.

Her mind suddenly filled with wild visions—of herself marched through the village by Watson, as she had once seen him march a poacher who had mauled one of Mr. Forrest's keepers—of the towering walls of Frampton jail—of a visible physical shame which would kill her—drive her mad. If, indeed, Isaac did not kill her before any one but he knew! He had been that cross and glum all these last weeks—never a bit of talk hardly—always snapping at her and the children. Yet he had never said a word to her about the drink—nor about the things she had bought. As to the "things" and the bills, she believed that he knew nothing—had noticed nothing. At home he was always smoking, sitting silent, with dim eyes, like a man in a dream—or reading his father's old books, "good books," which filled Bessie with a sense of dreariness unspeakable—or pondering his weekly paper.

But she believed he had begun to notice the drink. Drinking was universal in Clinton, though there was not much drunkenness. Teetotalers were unknown, and Isaac himself drank his beer freely, and a glass of spirits, like anybody else, on occasion. She had been used for years to fetch his beer from the public, and she had been careful. But there were signs— —

Oh! if she could only think of some way of putting it back—this thirty odd pounds. She held her head between her hands, thinking and thinking. Couldn't that little lawyer man to whom she went every month at Bedford, to fetch her legacy money—couldn't he lend it her, and keep her money till it was paid? She could make up a story, and give him something for himself to induce him to hold his tongue. She had thought of this often before, but never so urgently as now. She would take the carrier's cart to Bedford next day, while Isaac was at work, and try.

Yet all the time despair was at her heart. So hard to undo! Yet how easy it had been to take and to spend. She thought of that day in September, when she had got the news of her legacy—six shillings a week from an old aunt—her father's aunt, whose very existence she had forgotten. The wild delight of it! Isaac got sixteen shillings a week in wages—here was nearly half as much again. She was warned that it would come to an end in two years. But none the less it seemed to her a fortune—and all her life, before it came, mere hard pinching and endurance. She had always been one to spend where she could. Old John had often rated her for it. So had Isaac. But that was his money. This was hers, and he who, for religious reasons, had never made friends with or thought well of any of her family, instinctively disliked the money which had come from them, and made few inquiries into the spending of it.

Oh! the joy of those first visits to Frampton, when all the shops had seemed to be there for her, and she their natural mistress! How ready people had been to trust her in the village! How tempting it had been to brag and make a mystery! That old skinflint, Mrs. Moulsey, at "the shop," she had been all sugar and sweets *then*.

And a few weeks later—six, seven weeks later—about the beginning of October, these halcyon days had all come to an end. She owed what she could not pay—people had ceased to smile upon her—she was harassed, excited, worried out of her life.

Old familiar wonder of such a temperament! How can it be so easy to spend, so delightful to promise, and so unreasonably, so unjustly difficult, to pay?

She began to be mortally afraid of Isaac—of the effect of disclosures. One night she was alone in the cottage, almost beside herself under the pressure of one or two claims she could not meet—one claim especially, that of a little jeweller, from whom she had bought a gold ring and a brooch at Frampton—when the thought of John's hoard swept upon her—clutched her like something living and tyrannical, not to be shaken off.

It struck her all in an instant that there was another cupboard in the little parlour, exactly like that on the stairs. The lower cupboard had a key—what if it fitted?

The Devil must have been eager and active that night, for the key turned in the lock with a smoothness that made honesty impossible—almost foolish. And the old, weak lock on the box itself—why, a chisel had soon made an end of that! Only five minutes—it had been so quick—there had been no trouble. God had made no sign at all.

Since! All the village smiles—the village flatteries recovered—an orgie of power and pleasure—new passions and excitements—above all, the rising passion of drink, sweeping in storms through a weak nature that alternately opened to them and shuddered at them. And through everything the steadily dribbling away of the hoard—the astonishing ease and rapidity with which the coins—gold or silver—had flowed through her hands! How could one spend so much in meat and dress, in beer and gin, in giving other people beer and gin? How was it possible? She sat lost in miserable thoughts, a mist around her. . . .

"Wal, I niver!" said a low, astonished voice at the foot of the stairs.

Bessie rose to her feet with a shriek, the heart stopping in her breast. The door below was ajar, and through the opening peered a face—the vicious, drunken face of her husband's eldest son, Timothy Costrell.

The man below cast one more look of amazement at the woman standing on the top stair, at the candle behind her, at the open box. Then an idea struck him: he sprang up the stairs at a bound.

"By gosh!" he said, looking down at the gold and silver. *"By gosh!"*

Bessie tried to thrust him back. "What are you here for?" she asked fiercely, her trembling lips the colour of the whitewashed wall behind. "You get off at onst, or I'll call yer father."

He pushed her contemptuously aside. The swish of her dress caught the candle, and by good fortune put it out, or she would have been in a blaze. Now there was only the light from the paraffin lamp in the kitchen below striking upwards through the open door.

She fell against the doorway of her bedroom, panting and breathless, watching him.

He seated himself in her place, and stooped to look at the box. On the inside of the lid was pasted a discoloured piece of paper, and on the paper was written, in a round, laborious hand, the name, "John Bolderfield."

"My blazes!" he said slowly, his bloodshot eyes opening wider than ever. "It's old John's money! So yo've been after it, eh?"

He turned to her with a grin, one hand on the box. He had been tramping for more than three months, during which time they had heard nothing of him. His filthy clothes scarcely hung together. His cheeks were hollow and wolfish. From the whole man there rose a sort of exhalation of sodden vice. Bessie had seen him drunken and out at elbows before, but never so much of the beast as this.

However, by this time she had somewhat recovered herself, and, approaching him, she stooped and tried to shut the box.

"You take yourself off," she said, desperately, pushing him with her fist. "That money's no business o' yourn, It's John's, an' he's comin' back directly. He gave it us to look after, an' I wor countin' it. March!—there's your father comin'!"

And with all her force she endeavoured to wrench his hand away. He tore it from her, and hit out at her backwards—a blow that sent her reeling against the wall.

"Yo take yer meddlin' fist out o' that!" he said. "Father ain't coming, and if he wor, I 'spect I could manage the two on yer—*Keowntin'* it—" he mimicked her. "Oh! yer a precious innercent, ain't yer? But I know all about yer. Bless yer, I've been in at the Spotted Deer to-night, and there worn't nothin' else talked of but yo' and yor goin's on. There won't be a tongue in the place to-morrow that won't be a-waggin' about yer—yur a public charickter, yo' are—they'll be sendin' the reporters down on yer for a hinterview. 'Where the devil do she get the money?' they says."

He threw his curly head back and laughed till his sides shook.

"Lor', I didn't think I wor going to know quite so soon! An' sich queer 'arf-crowns, they ses, as she keeps a-changin'. Jarge somethin'—an old cove in a wig. An' 'ere they is, I'll be blowed—some on 'em. Well, yer a nice 'un, yer are!"

He stared her up and down with a kind of admiration.

Bessie began to cry feebly—the crying of a lost soul.

"Tim, if yer'll go away an' hold yer tongue, I'll give yer five o' them suverins, and not tell yer father nothin'."

"Five on 'em?" he said, grinning. "Five on 'em, eh?"

And, dipping his hands into the box, he began deliberately shovelling the whole hoard into his trousers and waist-coat pockets.

Bessie flung herself upon him. He gave her one business-like blow, which knocked her down against the bedroom door. The door yielded to her fall, and she lay there half stunned, the blood dripping from her temple.

"Noa, I'll not take 'em all," he said, not even troubling to look where she had fallen. "That 'ud be playing it rayther too low down on old John. I'll leave 'im two—jest two—for luck."

He buttoned up his coat tightly, then turned to throw a last glance at Bessie.

He had always disliked his father's second wife, and his sense of triumph was boundless.

"Oh! yer not hurt," he said; "yer shammin'. I advise yer to look sharp with shuttin' up. Father'll be up the hill in two or three minutes now. Sorry I can't 'elp yer, now yer've set me up so comfortabul. Bye-bye!"

He ran down the stairs. She, as her senses revived, heard him open the back-door, cross the little garden, and jump the hedge at the end of it.

Then she lay absolutely motionless, till suddenly there struck on her ear the distant sound of heavy steps. They roused her like a goad. She dragged herself to her feet, shut the box, had just time to throw it into the cupboard and lock the door, when she heard her husband walk into the kitchen. She crept into her own room, threw herself on the bed, and wrapped her head and eyes in an old shawl, shivering so that the mattresses shook.

"Bessie, where are yer?"

She did not answer. He made a sound of astonishment, and, finding no candle, took the lamp and mounted the stairs. They were covered with traces of muddy snow, and at the top he stooped to examine a spot upon the boards. It was blood; and his heart thumped in his breast.

"Bessie, whatever is the matter?"

For by this time he had perceived her on the bed. He put down the lamp and came to the bedside to look at her.

"I've 'ad a fall," she said, faintly. "I tripped up over my skirt as I wor comin' up to look at Arthur. My head's all bleedin'. Get me some water from over there."

His countenance fell sadly. But he got the water, exclaiming when he saw the wound.

He bathed it clumsily, then tied a bit of rag round it, and made her head easy with the pillow. She did not speak, and he sat on beside her, looking at her pale face, and torn, as the silent minutes passed, between conflicting impulses. He had just passed an hour listening to a good man's plain narrative of a life spent for Christ, amid fever-swamps, and human beings more deadly still. The vicar's friend was a missionary bishop, and a High Churchman; Isaac, as a staunch Dissenter by conviction and inheritance, thought ill both of bishops and Ritualists. Nevertheless, he had been touched; he had been fired. Deep, though often perplexed, instincts in his own heart had responded to the spiritual passion of the speaker. The religious atmosphere had stolen about him, melting and subduing.

And the first effect of it had been to quicken suddenly his domestic conscience; to make him think painfully of Bessie and the children as he climbed the hill. Was his wife going the way of his son? And he, sitting day after day like a dumb dog, instead of striving with her!

He made up his mind hurriedly. "Bessie," he said, stooping to her and speaking in a strange voice, "Bessie, had yer been to Dawson's?"

Dawson was the landlord of the Spotted Deer.

Bessie was long in answering. At last she said, almost inaudibly—

"Yes."

She fully understood what he had meant by the question, and she wondered whether he would fall into one of his rages and beat her.

Instead, his hand sought clumsily for hers.

"Bessie, yer shouldn't; yer mustn't do it no more; it'll make a bad woman of yer. I know as I'm not good to live with; I don't make things pleasant to yer; but I've been thinkin'; I'll try if yo'll try."

Bessie burst into tears. It seemed as though her life were breaking within her. Never since their early married days had he spoken to her like this. And she was in such piteous need of comfort; of some strong hand to help her out of the black pit in which she lay. The wild impulse crossed her to sit up and tell him—to throw it all on Timothy, to show him the cupboard and the box. Should she tell him; brave it all now that he was like this? Between them they might find a way—make it good.

Then the thought of the man in the public-house, of the half-crowns, a host of confused and guilty memories, swept upon her. How could she ever get herself out of it? Her heart beat so that it seemed a live creature strangling and silencing her. She was still fighting with her tears and her terror when she heard Isaac say—

"I know yer'll try, and I'll help yer. I'll be a better husband to yer, I swear I will. Give us a kiss, old woman."

She turned her face, sobbing, and he kissed her cheek.

Then she heard him say in another tone—

"An' I got a bit o' news down at the Club as will liven yer up. Parkinson was there; just come over from Frampton to see his mother; an' he says John will be here to-morrer or next day. 'Ee seed him yesterday—pulled down dreadful—quite the old man, 'ee says. An' John told him as he was comin' 'ome directly to live comfortable."

Bessie drew her shawl over her head.

"To-morrer, did yer say?" she asked in a whisper.

"Mos' like. Now, you go to sleep; I'll put out the lamp."

But all night long Bessie lay wide awake in torment, her soul hardening within her, little by little.

SCENE IV

Just before dark on the following day a man descended from a down train at the Clinton Magna station. The porters knew him and greeted him; so did one or two labourers outside, as he set off to walk to the village, which was about a mile distant.

"Well, John, so yer coom back," said one of them, an old man, grasping the newcomer by the hand. "An' I can't say as yer looks is any credit to Frampton—no, that aa can't."

John, indeed, wore a sallow and pinched air, and walked lamely, with a stick.

"Noa," he said peevishly; "it's a beastly place is Frampton; a damp, nassty hole as iver I saw—gives yer the rheumaticks to look at it. I've 'ad a doose of a time, I 'ave, I can tell yer—iver sense I went. But I'll pull up now."

"Aye, this air 'll do yer," said the other. "Where are yer stoppin'? Costrells'?"

John nodded.

"They don't know nothin' about my comin', but I dessay they'll find me somethin' to sleep on. I'll 'ave my own place soon, and some one to look arter it."

He drew himself up involuntarily, with the dignity that waits on property. A laugh, rather jeering than cordial, ran through the group of labourers.

"Aye, yer'll be livin' at your ease," said the man who had spoken first. "When will yo' give us a drink, yer lardship?"

The others grinned.

"Where's your money, John?" said a younger man, suddenly staring hard at the returned wanderer.

John started.

"Don't you talk your nonsense!" he said fretfully; "an' I must be getting on, afore dark."

He went his way, but, as he turned a corner of the road, he saw them still standing where he had left them. They seemed to be watching his progress, which astonished him.

A light of windy sunset lay spread over the white valley, and the freshening gusts drove the powdery snow before them, and sent little stabs of pain through John's shrinking body. Yet how glad he was to find himself again between those familiar hedges, to see the church-tower in front of him, the long hill to his right!

His heart swelled at once with longing and satisfaction. During his Frampton job, and in the infirmary, he had suffered much, physically and mentally. He had missed Eliza and the tendance of years more than he had ever imagined he could; and he had found himself too old for new faces and a new society. When he fell ill he had been sorely tempted to send for some of his money, and get himself nursed and cared for at the respectable lodging where he had put up. But no; in the end he set his teeth and went into the infirmary. He had planned not to touch his hoard till he had done with the Frampton job and returned to Clinton for good. His peasant obstinacy could not endure to be beaten; nor, indeed, could he bring himself to part with his keys, to trust the opening of the hoard even to Isaac.

Since then he had passed through many weary weeks, sometimes of acute pain, sometimes of sinking weakness, during which he had been haunted by many secret torments, springing mainly from the fear of death. He had almost been driven to make his will. But in the end superstitious reluctance prevailed. He had not made his will; and to dwell on the fact gave him the sensation of having escaped a bond, if not a danger. He did not want to leave his money behind him; he wanted to spend it, as he had told Eliza and Mary Anne and Bessie scores of times. To have assigned it to any one else, even after his death, would have made it less his own.

Ah, well! those bad weeks were done, and here he was, at home again. Suddenly, as he tramped on, he caught sight against the hill of Bessie's cottage, the blue smoke from it blown across the rime-laden trees behind it. He drew in his breath with a deep, tremulous delight. That buoyant self-congratulation indeed which had stood between him and the pain of Eliza's death was gone. Rather, there was in him a profound yearning for rest, for long dreaming by the fire or in the sun, with his pipe to smoke, and Jim's Louisa to look after him, and nothing to do but to draw a half-crown from his box when he wanted it. No more hard work in rain and cold; and no cringing, either, to the young and prosperous for the mere fault of age. The snowy valley, with its circling woods, opened to him like a mother's breast; the sight of it filled him with a hundred simple hopes and consolations; he hurried to bury himself in it and be at peace.

He was within a hundred yards of the first house in the village, when he saw a tall figure in uniform approaching, and recognised Watson.

At sight of him the policeman stopped short, and John was conscious of a moment's vague impression of something strange in Watson's looks.

However, Watson shook hands with great friendliness.

"Well, I'm glad to see yer, John, I'm sure. An' now, I s'pose, you're back for good?"

"Aye. I'm not going away no more. I've done my share—I wants a bit o' rest."

"Of course yer do. You've been ill, 'aven't yer? You look like it. An' yer puttin' up at Costrells'?"

"Yes, till I can turn round a bit. 'Ave yer seen any thin' ov 'em? 'Ow's Bessie?"

Watson faced back towards the village.

"I'll walk with yer a bit—I'm in no 'urry. Oh, she's all right. You 'eard of her bit o' money?"

John opened his eyes.

"Noa, I don' know as I did."

"It wor an aunt o' hers, soa I understan'—quite a good bit o' money."

"Did yer iver hear the name?" said John, eagerly.

"Some one livin' at Bedford, I did 'ear say."

John laughed, not without good-humoured relief. It would have touched his vanity had his niece been discovered to be richer than himself.

"Oh, that's old Sophy Clarke!" he said. "Her 'usband bought the lease o' two little 'ouses in Church Street, and they braat 'er in six shillin's a week for years, an' she allus said she'd leave it to Bessie if she wor took afore the lease wor up. But the lease ull be up end o' next year, I know, for I saw the old lady myself last Michaelmas twelve-month, an' she told me all about it, though I worn't to tell nobody meself. An' I didn't know Sophy wor gone. Ah, well! it's not much, but it's 'andy—it's 'andy."

"Six shillin's a week!" said Watson, raising his eyebrows. "It's a nice bit o' money while it lassts, but I'd ha' thought Mrs. Costrell 'ad come into a deal more nor that."

"Oh, but she's sich a one to spend, is Bessie!" said John, anxiously. "It's surprisin' 'ow the money runs. It's sixpence 'ere, an' sixpence there, allus dribblin', an' dribblin', out ov 'er. I've allus tole 'er as she'll end 'er days on the parish."

"Sixpences!" said Watson, with a laugh. "It's not sixpences as Mrs. Costrell's 'ad the spendin' of this last month or two—it's *suverins*—an' plenty ov 'em. You may be sure you've got the wrong tale about the money, John; it wor a deal more nor you say."

John stood stock still at the word "sovereigns," his jaw dropping.

"*Suverins*," he said trembling; "suverins? Bessie ain't got no suverins. Isaac arns sixteen shillin' a week."

The colour was ebbing fast from his cheek and lips. Watson threw him a quick, professional glance, then rapidly consulted with himself. No; he decided to hold his tongue.

"Yo' *are* reg'lar used up," he said, taking hold of the old fellow kindly by the arm. "Shall I walk yer up the hill?"

John withdrew himself.

"*Suverins!*" he repeated, in a low, hoarse voice. "She ain't got 'em, I tell yer—she ain't got 'em!"

The last words rose to a sort of cry, and, without another word to Watson, the old man started at a feeble run, his head hanging.

Watson followed him, afraid lest he should drop in the road. Instead, John seemed to gather strength. He made straight for the hill, taking no heed whatever of two or three startled acquaintances who stopped and shouted to him. When the ground began to rise he stumbled again and again, but, by a marvel, did not fall, and his pace hardly slackened. Watson had difficulty in keeping up with him.

But when the policeman reached his own cottage on the side of the road, he stopped, panting, and contented himself with looking after the mounting figure. As soon as it turned the corner of the Costrells' lane, he went into his own house, said a word to his wife, and sat himself down at his own back door to await events—to ponder, also, a few conversations he had held that morning, with Mrs. Moulsey at "the shop," with Dawson, with Hall the butcher. Poor old John—poor old fellow!

When Bolderfield reached the paling in front of the Costrells' cottage, he paused a moment, holding for support to the half-open gate and struggling for breath. "I must keep my 'edd, I must," he was saying to himself piteously; "don' yer be a fool, John Borroful, don' yer be a fool!"

As he stood there, a child's face pushed the window-blind of the cottage aside, and the lame boy's large eyes looked Bolderfield up and down. Immediately after, the door opened, and all four children stood huddling behind each other on the threshold. They all looked shyly at the newcomer. They knew him, but in six months they had grown strange to him.

"Arthur, where's your mother?" said John, at last able to walk firmly up to the door.

"Don' know."

"When did yer see her lasst?"

"She wor 'ere gettin' us our tea," said another child; "but she didn't eat nothin'."

John impatiently pushed the children before him back into the kitchen.

"You 'old your tongues," he said, "an' stay 'ere."

And he made for the door in the kitchen wall. But Arthur caught hold of his coat tails and clung to them.

"Yer oughtn't to go up there—mother don't let any one go there."

John wrenched himself violently away.

"Oh, don't she! yo' take your 'ands away, yer little varmint, or I'll brain yer."

He raised his stick, threatening. The child, terrified, fell back, and John, opening the door, rushed up the stairs.

He was so terribly excited that his fumbling fingers could hardly find the ribbon round his neck. At last he drew it over his head, and made stupendous efforts to steady his hand sufficiently to put the key in the lock.

The children below heard a sharp cry directly the cupboard door was opened; then the frantic dragging of a box on to the stairs, the creak of hinges—a groan long and lingering—and then silence.

They clung together in terror, and the little girls began to cry. At last Arthur took courage and opened the door.

The old man was sitting on the top stair, supported sideways by the wall, his head hanging forward, and his hands dropping over his knees, in a dead faint.

At the sight all four children ran helter-skelter into the lane, shouting "Mammy! mammy!" in an anguish of fright. Their clamour was caught by the fierce north wind, which had begun to sweep the hill, and was borne along till it reached the ears of a woman who was sitting sewing in a cottage some fifty yards further up the lane. She stepped to her door, opened it and listened.

"It's at Bessie's," she said; "whativer's wrong wi' the childer?"

By this time Arthur had begun to run towards her. Darkness was falling rapidly, but she could distinguish his small figure against the snow, and his halting gait.

"What is it, Arthur?—what is it, lammie?"

"O Cousin Mary Anne! Cousin Mary Anne! It's Uncle John, an' 'ee's dead!"

She ran like the wind at the words, catching at the child's hand in the dark, and dragging him along with her.

"Where is he, Arthur?—don't take on, honey!"

The child hurried on with her, sobbing, and she was soon on the stairs beside the unconscious John.

Mary Anne looked with amazement at the cupboard and the open box. Then she laid the old man on the floor, her gentle face working with the effort to remember what the doctor had once told her of the best way of dealing with persons in a faint. She got water, and she sent Arthur to a neighbour for brandy.

"Where's your mother, child?" she asked, as she despatched him.

"Don' know," repeated the boy, stupidly.

"Oh, for goodness' sake, she's never at Dawson's again!" groaned Mary Anne to herself; "she wor there last night, an' the night afore that. And her mother's brother lyin' like this in 'er house!"

He was so long in coming round that her ignorance began to fear the worst. But, just as she was telling the eldest girl to put on her hat and jacket and run for the doctor, poor John revived.

He struggled to a sitting posture, looked wildly at her and at the box. As his eye caught the two sovereigns still lying at the bottom, he gave a cry of rage, and got upon his feet with a mighty effort.

"Where's Bessie, I tell yer? Where's the huzzy gone? I'll have the law on 'er! I'll make 'er give it up—by the Lord I will!"

"John, what is it? John, my dear!" cried Mary Anne, supporting him, and terrified lest he should pitch headlong down the stairs.

"Yo' 'elp me down," he said violently. "We'll find 'er—we'll wring it out ov 'er—the mean, thievin' vagabond! Changin' suverins, 'as she? We'll soon know about that—yo' 'elp me down, I tell yer."

And, with her assistance, he hobbled down the stairs, hardly able to stand. Mary Anne's eyes were starting out of her head with fear and agitation, and the children were staring at the old man as he came tottering into the kitchen, when a sound at the outer door made them all turn.

The door opened, and Bessie appeared on the threshold.

At sight of her John seemed to lose his senses. He rushed at her, threatening, imploring, reviling—while Mary Anne could only cling to his arms and coat, lest he should attempt some bodily mischief.

Bessie closed the door, leant against it, and folded her arms. She was white and haggard, but perfectly cool. In this moment of excitement it struck neither John nor Mary Anne—nor, indeed, herself—that her manner, with its brutality, and its poorly feigned surprise, was the most revealing element in the situation.

"What's all this about yer money?" she said, staring John in the face. "What do I know about yer money? 'Ow dare yer say such things? I 'aven't anythin' to do with it, an' never 'ad."

He raved at her, in reply, about the position in which he had found the box— on the top of its fellow instead of underneath, where he had placed it—about the broken lock, the sovereigns she had been changing, and the things Watson had said of her—winding up with a peremptory demand for his money.

"Yo' gi' me my money back," he said, holding out a shaking hand. "Yer can't 'ave spent it all—'tain't possible—an' yer ain't chucked it out o' winder. Yer've got it somewhere 'idden, an' I'll get it out o' you if I die for 't!"

Bessie surveyed him steadily. She had not even flinched at the mention of the sovereigns.

"What yer 'aven't got, yer can't give," she said. "I don' know nothin' about it, an' I've tole yer. There's plenty o' bad people in the world—beside me. Some-body came in o' nights, I suppose, an' picked the lock—there's many as 'ud think nothin' of it. And it 'ud be easy done—we all sleeps 'ard."

"Bessie!" cried Mary Anne, outraged by something in her tone, "aren't yer sorry for 'im?"

She pointed to the haggard and trembling man.

Bessie turned to her reluctantly. "Aye, I'm sorry," she said sullenly. "But he shouldn't fly out at yer without 'earin' a word. 'Ow should I know anythin' about his money? 'Ee locked it up hisself, an' tuk the keys."

"An' them suverins," roared John, rattling his stick on the floor; "where did yer get them suverins?"

"I got 'em from old Sophy Clarke—leastways, from Sophy Clarke's lawyer. And it ain't no business o' yourn."

At this John fell into a frenzy, shouting at her in inarticulate passion, calling her liar and thief.

She fronted it with perfect composure. Her fine eyes blazed, but otherwise her face might have been a waxen mask. With her, in this scene, was all the tragic dignity; with him, the weakness and vulgarity.

At last the little widow caught her by the arm, and drew her from the door.

"Let me take 'im to my place," she pleaded: "it's no good talkin' while 'ee's like 'ee is—not a bit o' good. John—John, dear! you come along wi' me. Shall I get Saunders to come an' speak to yer?"

A gleam of sudden hope shot into the old man's face. He had not thought of Saunders; but Saunders had a head; he might unravel this accursed thing.

"Aye!" he said, lurching forward, "let's find Saunders—coom along—let's find Saunders."

Mary Anne guided him through the door, Bessie standing aside. As the widow passed, she touched Bessie piteously.

"Oh, Bessie, yer *didn't* do it—say yer didn't!"

Bessie looked at her dry-eyed and contemptuous. Something in the speaker's emotion seemed to madden her.

"Don't yer be a fool, Mary Anne—that's all!" she said scornfully, and Mary Anne fled from her.

When the door had closed upon them Bessie came up to the fire, her teeth chattering. She sank down in front of it, spreading out her hands. The children silently crowded up to her; first she pushed them away, then she caught at the child nearest to her, pressed its fair head against her, then again roughly put it aside. She was accustomed to chatter with them, scold them and slap them; but to-night they were uneasily dumb. They looked at her with round eyes; and at last their looks annoyed her. She told them to go to bed, and they slunk away, gaping at the open box on the stairs, and huddling together overhead, all on one bed, in the bitter cold, to whisper to each other. Isaac was a stern parent; Bessie a capricious one; and the children, though they could be riotous enough by themselves, were nervous and easily cowed at home.

Bessie, left alone, sat silently over the fire, her thin lips tight-set. She would deny everything—*everything*. Let them find out what they could. Who could prove what was in John's box when he left it? Who could prove she hadn't got those half-crowns in change somewhere?

The reflection of the day had only filled her with a passionate and fierce regret. *Why* had she not followed her first impulse and thrown it all on Timothy?—told the story to Isaac while she was still bleeding from his son's violence? It had been her only chance, and out of pure stupidness she had lost it. To have grasped it might at least have made him take her part, if it had forced him to give up Timothy. And who would have listened to Timothy's tales?

She sickened at the thought of her own folly, beating her knee with her clenched fist. For, to tell the tale now would only be to make her doubly vile in Isaac's eyes. He would not believe her—no one would believe her. What motive could she plead for her twenty-four hours of silence, she knowing that John was coming back immediately? Isaac would only hate her for throwing it on Timothy.

Then again, the memory of the half-crowns, and the village talk—and Watson—would close upon her, putting her in a cold sweat.

When would Isaac come? Who would tell him? As she looked forward to the effect upon him, all her muscles stiffened. If he drove her to it, aye, she *would* tell him—she didn't care a ha'porth, she vowed. If he must have it, let him. But as the name of Isaac, the thought of Isaac, hovered in her brain, she must needs brush away wild tears. That morning, for the first time for months, he had been so kind to her and the children, so chatty and cheerful.

Distant steps along the lane! She sprang to her feet, ran into the back kitchen, tied on her apron, hastily filled an earthenware bowl with water from the pump, and, carrying it back to the front kitchen, began to wash up the tea-things, making a busy household clatter as she slid them into the bowl.

A confused sound of feet approached the house, and there was a knock.

"Come in," said Bessie.

Three figures appeared, the huge form of Saunders the smith in front, John and Mary Anne Waller behind.

Saunders took off his cap politely. The sight of his bald head, his double chin, his mouth with its queer twitch, which made him seem as though perpetually about to laugh, if he had not perpetually thought better of it, filled Bessie with angry excitement. She barely nodded to him, in reply to his greeting.

"May we come in, Mrs. Costrell?" Saunders inquired, in his most deliberate voice.

"If yer want to," said Bessie, shortly, taking out a cup and drying it.

Saunders drew in the other two and shut the door.

"Sit down, John. Sit down, Mrs. Waller."

John did as he was told. Dishevelled and hopeless misery spoke in his stained face, his straggling hair, his shirt burst open at the neck and showing his wrinkled throat. But he fixed his eyes passionately on Saunders, thirsting for every word.

"Well, Mrs. Costrell," said Saunders, settling himself comfortably, "you'll be free to confess, won't yer, this is an oogly business—a very oogly business? Now, will yer let us ask yer a question or two?"

"I dessay," said Bessie, polishing her cup.

"Well, then—to begin reg'lar, Mrs. Costrell—yo' agree, don't yer, as Muster Bolderfield put his money in your upstairs cupboard?"

"I agree as he put his box there"—said Bessie, sharply.

John broke into inarticulate and abusive clamour. Bessie turned upon him.

"'Ow did any of us know what yer'd got in your box? Did yer ever show it to me, or Mary Anne there, or any livin' soul in Clinton? Did yer?"

She waited, hawk-like, for the answer.

"Did yer, John?" repeated Saunders, judicially.

John groaned, rocking himself to and fro.

"Noa. I niver did—I niver did," he said. "Nobbut to Eliza—an' she's gone—she's gone!"

"Keep your 'ead, John," said Saunders, putting out a calming hand. "Let's get to the bottom o' this, quiet an' *reg'lar*. An' yer didn't tell any one 'ow much yer 'ad?"

"Nobbut Eliza—nobbut Eliza!" said the old man again.

"Yer didn't tell *me*, I know," said Saunders, blandly.

John seemed to shrink together under the smith's glance. If only he had not been a jealous fool, and had left it with Saunders.

Saunders, however, refrained for the present from drawing his self-evident moral. He sat twirling his cap between his knees, and his shrewd eye travelled round the kitchen, coming back finally to Bessie, who was washing and drying diligently. As he watched her cool movements Saunders felt the presence of an enemy worthy of his steel, and his emulation rose.

"I understan', Mrs. Costrell," he said, speaking with great civility, "as the cupboard where John put his money is a cupboard *hon* the stairs? Not in hany room, but *hon* the stairs? Yer'll kindly correck me if I say anythin' wrong."

Bessie nodded.

"Aye—top o' the stairs—right-'and side," groaned John.

"An' John locked it hisself, an' tuk the key?" Saunders proceeded.

John plucked at his neck again, and, dumbly, held out the key.

"An' there worn't nothin' wrong wi' the lock when yo' opened it, John?"

"Nothin', Muster Saunders—I'll take my davy."

Saunders ruminated.

"Theer's a cupboard there," he said suddenly, raising his hand and pointing to the cupboard beside the fireplace. "Is't anythin' like the cupboard on th' stairs, John?"

"Aye, 'tis!" said John, startled and staring. "Aye, 'tis, Muster Saunders!"

Saunders rose.

"Per'aps," he said slowly, "Mrs. Costrell will do us the favour ov lettin' us hexamine that 'ere cupboard?"

He walked across to it. Bessie's hand dropped; she turned sharply, supporting herself against the table, and watched him, her chest heaving.

"There's no key 'ere," said Saunders, stooping to look at the lock. "Try yours, John."

John rushed forward, but Bessie put herself in the way.

"What are yer meddlin' with my 'ouse for?" she said fiercely. "Just mek your-selves scarce, all the lot o' yer! I don't know nothin' about his money, an' I'll not have yer *insultin'* me in me own place! Get out o' my kitchen, if *yo'* please!"

Saunders buttoned his coat.

"Sartinly, Mrs. Costrell, sartinly," he said, with emphasis. "Come along, John. Yer must get Watson and put it in 'is hands. 'Ee's the law, is Watson. Maybe as Mrs. Costrell 'ull listen to *'im.*"

Mary Anne ran to Bessie in despair.

"Oh, Bessie, Bessie, my dear—don't let 'em get Watson; let 'em look into 't theirselves—it'll be better for yer, my dear, it *will.*"

Bessie looked from one to the other, panting. Then she turned back to the table.

"*I* don' care what they do," she said, with sullen passion. "I'm not stannin' in any one's way, I tell yer. The more they finds out the better I'm pleased."

The look of incipient laughter on Saunders's countenance became more pro-nounced—that is to say, the left-hand corner of his mouth twitched a little higher. But it was rare for him to complete the act, and he was not in the least minded to do so now. He beckoned to John, and John, trembling, took off his keys and gave them to him, pointing to that which belonged to the treasure cupboard.

Saunders slipped it into the lock before him. It moved with ease, backwards and forwards.

"H'm! that's strange," he said, taking out the key and turning it over thought-fully in his hand. "Yer didn't think as there were *another* key in this 'ouse that would open your cupboard, did yer, Bolderfield?"

The old man sank weeping on a chair. He was too broken, too exhausted, to revile Bessie any more.

"Yo' tell her, Muster Saunders," he said, "to gie it me back! I'll not ast for all on it, but some on it, Muster Saunders—some on it. She *can't* 'a spent it. She must 'a got it somewhere. Yo' speak to her, Muster Saunders. It's a crule thing to rob an old man like me—an' her own mother's brother. Yo' speak to 'er—an' yo', too, Mary Anne."

He looked piteously from one to the other. But his misery only seemed to goad Bessie to fresh fury. She turned upon him, arms akimbo.

"Oh! an' of course it must be *me* as robs yer! It couldn't be nobody else, could it? There isn't tramps, an' thieves, an' rogues—'undreds of 'em—going about o' nights? Nary one, I believe yer! There isn't another thief in Clinton Magna, nob-but Bessie Costrell, is ther? But yer'll not blackguard me for nothin', I can tell yer.

Now will yer jest oblige me by takin' yourselves off? I shall 'ave to clean up after yer" — she pointed scornfully to the marks of their muddy boots on the floor — "an' it's gettin' late."

"One moment, Mrs. Costrell," said Saunders, gently rubbing his hands. "With your leave, John and I 'ull just inspeck the cupboard _hup_stairs before leavin' — an' then we'll clear out double quick. But we'll 'ave one try if we can't 'it on somethin' as 'ull show 'ow the thief got in — with your leave, of *coorse*."

Bessie hesitated; then she threw some spoons she held into the water beside her with a violent gesture.

"Go where yer wants," she said, and returned to her washing.

Saunders began to climb the narrow stairs, with John behind him. But the smith's small eyes had a puzzled look.

"There's *somethin'* rum," he said to himself. "'Ow *did* she spend it all? 'As she been carryin' on with some one be'ind Isaac's back, or is Isaac in it too? It's one or t'other."

Meanwhile, Bessie, left behind, was consumed by a passionate effort of memory. *What* had she done with the key the night before, after she had locked the cupboard? Her brain was blurred. The blow — the fall — seemed to have confused even the remembrance of the scene with Timothy. How was it, for instance, that she had put the box back in the wrong place? She put her hand to her head, trying in an anguish to recollect the exact details.

The little widow sat, meanwhile, a few yards away, her thin hands clasped on her lap in her usual attitude of humble entreaty; her soft, grey eyes, brimmed with tears, were fixed on Bessie. Bessie did not know that she was there — that she existed.

The door had closed after the two men. Bessie could hear vague movements, but nothing more. Presently she could bear it no longer. She went to the door and opened it.

She was just in time. By the light of the bit of candle that John held, she saw Saunders sitting on the stair, the shadow of his huge frame thrown black on the white wall; she saw him stoop suddenly, as a bird pounces; she heard an exclamation — then a sound of metal.

Her involuntary cry startled the men above.

"All right, Mrs. Costrell," said Saunders, briskly — "all right. We'll be down directly."

She came back into the kitchen, a mist before her eyes, and fell heavily on a chair by the fire. Mary Anne approached her, only to be pushed back. The widow stood listening, in an agony.

It took Saunders a minute or two to complete his case. Then he slowly descended the stairs, carrying the box, his great weight making the house shake. He entered the kitchen first, John behind him. But at the same moment that they appeared the outer door opened, and Isaac Costrell, preceded by a gust of snow, stood on the threshold.

"Why, John!" he cried, in amazement—"an' *Saunders*!"

He looked at them, then at Mary Anne, then at his wife.

There was an instant's dead silence. Then the tottering John came forward.

"An' I'm glad yer come, Isaac, that I am—thankful! Now yer can tell me what yer wife's done with my money. D'yer mind that box? It wor you an' I carried it across that night as Watson come out on us. An' yo'll bear me witness as we locked it up, an' yo' saw me tie the two keys roun' my neck—yo' *did*, Isaac. An' now, Isaac,"—the hoarse voice began to tremble—"now there's two—suverins—left, and one 'arf-crown—out o' seventy-one pound fower an' sixpence—seventy-one pound, Isaac! Yo'll get it out on 'er, Isaac, yer will, won't yer?"

He looked up, imploring.

Isaac, after the first violent start, stood absolutely motionless, Saunders observing him. As one of the main props of Church Establishment in the village, Saunders had no great opinion of Isaac Costrell, who stood for the dissidence of dissent. The two men had never been friends, and Saunders, in this affair, had, perhaps, exercised the quasi-judicial functions the village had long, by common consent, allowed him, with more readiness than usual.

As soon as John ceased speaking Isaac walked up to Saunders.

"Let me see that box," he said peremptorily. "Put it down."

Saunders, who had rested the box on the back of a chair, placed it gently on the table, assisted by Isaac. A few feet away stood Bessie, saying nothing, her hand holding the duster on her hip, her eyes following her husband.

He looked carefully at the two sovereigns lying on the bit of old cloth which covered the bottom of the box, and the one half-crown that Timothy had forgotten; he took up the bit of cloth and shook it, he felt along the edge of the box, he examined the wrenched lock.

Then he stood for an instant, his hand on the box, his eyes staring straight before him in a kind of dream.

Saunders grew impatient. He pushed John aside, and came to the table, leaning his hands upon it so as to command Isaac's face.

"Now look 'ere, Isaac," he said, in a different voice from any that he had yet employed, "let's come to business. These 'ere are the facks o' this case, and 'ow we're agoin' to get over 'em I don't see. John leaves his money in your cupboard. Yo' an' he lock it up, an' John goes away with 'is keys 'ung roun' 'is neck. Yo' agree to that? Well an' good. But there's *another* key in your 'ouse, Isaac, as opens John's cupboard. Ah——"

He waved his hand in deprecation of Isaac's movement.

"I dessay yo' didn't know nowt about it—that's noather 'ere nor there. Yo' try John's key in that there door"—he pointed to the cupboard by the fire—"an' yo'll find it fits *ex* — act. Then, thinks I, where's the key as belongs to that 'ere cupboard? An' John an' I goes upstairs to look about us, an' in noa time at aw, I sees a 'ole in the skirtin'. I whips in my finger — lor' bless yer! I knew it wor there the moment I sets eyes on the hole."

He held up the key triumphantly. By this time, no Old Bailey lawyer making a hanging speech could have had more command of his task.

"'Ere then we 'ave" — he checked the items off on his fingers — "box locked up — key in the 'ouse as fits it, unbeknown to John — money tuk out — key 'idden away. But that's not all — not by long chalks — there's another side to the affair _hal_together."

Saunders drew himself up, thrust his hands deep into his pockets, and cleared his throat.

"Perhaps yer don' know — I'm sartin sure yer don' know — leastways I'm hinclined that way, — as Mrs. Costrell" — he made a polite inclination towards Bessie — "'ave been makin' free with money — fower — five — night a week at the Spotted Deer — fower — five — night a week. She'd used to treat every young feller, an' plenty old 'uns too, as turned up; an' there was a many as only went to Dawson's becos they knew as she'd treat 'em. Now, she didn't go on tick at Dawson's; she'd *pay*, — an' she allus payed in 'arf-crowns. An' those 'arf-crowns were curious 'arf-crowns; an' it came into Dawson's 'ead as he'd colleck them 'arf-crowns. 'Ee wanted to see summat, 'ee said — an' I dessay 'ee did. An' people began to taak. Last night theer wor a bit of a roompus, it seems, while Mrs. Costrell was a-payin' another o' them things, an' summat as was said come to my ears — an' come to Watson's. An' me an' Watson 'ave been makin' inquiries — an' Mr. Dawson wor obligin' enough to make me a small loan, 'ee wor. Now, I've got just one question to ask o' John Borroful."

He put his hand into his waistcoat pocket, and drew out a silver coin.

"Is that yourn, John?"

John fell upon it with a cry.

"Aye, Saunders, it's mine. Look ye 'ere, Isaac, it's a king's 'ead. It's Willum — not Victory. I saved that 'un up when I wor a lad at Mason's — an' look yer, there's my mark in the corner — every 'arf-crown I ever 'ad I marked like that."

He held it under Isaac's staring eyes, pointing to the little scratched cross in the corner.

"'Ere's another, John — two on 'em," said Saunders, pulling out a second and a third.

John, in a passion of hope, identified them both.

"Then," said Saunders, slapping the table solemnly, "theer's nobbut one more thing to say — an' sorry I am to say it. Them coins, Isaac" — he pointed a slow finger at Bessie, whose white, fierce face moved involuntarily — "them 'arf-crowns wor paid across the bar lasst night, or the night afore, at Dawson's, by *yor wife*, as is now stannin' there, an' she'll deny it if she can!"

For an instant the whole group preserved their positions—the breath suspended on their lips.

Then Isaac strode up to his wife, and gripped her by the arms.

"Did yer do it?" he asked her.

He held her, looking into her eyes. Slowly she sank away from him; she would have fallen, but for a chair that stood beside her.

"Oh, yer brute!" she said, turning her head to Saunders an instant, and speaking under her breath, with a kind of sob. "Yer *brute!*"

Isaac walked to the door, and threw it open.

"Per'aps yer'll go," he said grimly.

And the three went, without a word.

SCENE V

So the husband and wife were left together in the cottage room. The door had no sooner closed on Saunders and his companions than Isaac was seized with that strange sense of walking amid things unreal upon a wavering earth which is apt to beset the man who has any portion of the dreamer's temperament under any sudden rush of circumstance. He drew his hand across his brow, bewildered. The fire leapt and chattered in the grate; the newly-washed tea-things on the table shone under the lamp; the cat lay curled, as usual, on the chair where he sat after supper to read his *Christian World*; yet all things were not the same. What had changed?

Then, across poor John's rifled box, he saw his wife sitting rigid on the chair where he had left her.

He came and sat down at the corner of the table, close to her, his chin on his hand.

"'Ow did yer spend it?" he said, startled, as the words came out, by his own voice, so grinding and ugly was the note of it.

Her miserable eyes travelled over his face, seeking, as it were, for some promise, however faint, of future help and succour, however distant.

Apparently she saw none, for her own look flamed to fresh defiance.

"I didn't spend it. Saunders wor lyin'."

"'Ow did yer get them half-crowns?"

"I got 'em at Bedford. Mr. Grimstone give 'em me."

Isaac looked at her hard, his shame burning into his heart. This was how she had got her money for the gin. Of course, she had lied to him the night before, in her account of her fall, and of that mark on her forehead, which still showed, a red disfigurement, under the hair she had drawn across it. The sight of it, of her, began to excite in him a quick loathing. He was at bottom a man of violent passions, and, in the presence of evil-doing so flagrant, so cruel—of a household ruin so complete—his religion failed him.

"When was it as yer opened that box fust?" he asked her again, scorning her denials.

She burst into a rage of tears, lifting her apron to her eyes, and flinging names at him that he scarcely heard.

There was a little cold tea in a cup close to him that Bessie had forgotten. He stretched out his hand, and took a mouthful, moistening his dry lips and throat.

"Yer'll go to prison for this," he said, jerking it out as he put the cup down.

He saw her shiver. Her nerve was failing her. The convulsive sobs continued, but she ceased to abuse him. He wondered when he should be able to get it out of her. He himself could no more have wept than iron and fire weep.

"Are yer goin' to tell me when yer took that money, and 'ow yer spent it? 'Cos if yer don't, I shall go to Watson."

Even in her abasement it struck her as shameful, unnatural, that he, her husband, should say this. Her remorse returned upon her heart, like a tide driven back. She answered him not a word.

He put his silver watch on the table.

"I'll give yer two minutes," he said.

There was silence in the cottage except for the choking, hysterical sounds she could not master. Then he took up his hat again, and went out into the snow, which was by now falling fast.

She remained helpless and sobbing, unconscious of the passage of time, one hand playing incessantly with a child's comforter that lay beside her on the table, the other wiping away the crowding tears. But her mind worked feverishly all the time, and gradually she fought herself free of this weeping, which clutched her against her will.

Isaac was away for an hour. When he came back, he closed the door carefully, and, walking to the table, threw down his hat upon it. His face under its ruddy brown had suffered some radical, disintegrating change.

"They've traced yer," he said hoarsely; "they've got it up to twenty-six pound, an' more. Most on it 'ere in Clinton—some on it, Muster Miles, o' Frampton, 'ull swear to. Watson 'ull go over to Frampton, for the warrant—to-morrer."

The news shook her from head to foot. She stared at him wildly—speechless.

"But that's not 'arf," he went on—"not near 'arf. Do yer 'ear? What did yer do with the rest? I'll not answer for keepin' my 'ands off yer if yer won't tell."

In his trance of rage and agony, he was incapable of pity. He had small need to threaten her with blows—every word stabbed.

But her turn had come to strike back. She raised her head; she measured her news against his; and she did it with a kind of exultation.

"Then I *will* tell yer—an' I 'ope it 'ull do yer good. *I* took thirty-one pound o' Bolderfield's money then—but it warn't me took the rest. Some one else tuk it, an' I stood by an' saw 'im. When I tried to stop 'im—look 'ere."

She raised her hand, nodding, and pointing to the wound on her brow.

Isaac leant heavily on the table. A horrible suspicion swept through him. Had she wronged him in a yet blacker way? He bent over her, breathing fast—ready to strike.

"Who was it?"

She laughed. "Well, it wor *Timothy*, then—yur precious—beautiful son—Timothy!"

He fell back.

"Yo're lyin'," he cried; "yer want to throw it off on some one. How cud Timothy 'ave 'ad anythin' to do with John's money? Timothy's not been near the place this three months."

"Not till lasst night," she said, mocking him. "I'll grant yer—not till lasst night. But it *do* 'appen, as lasst night Timothy took forty-one pound o' John Borroful's money out o' that box, an got off—clean. I'm sorry if yer don't like it—but I can't 'elp that; yo' listen 'ere."

And, lifting a quivering finger, she told her tale at last, all the beginning of it confused and almost unintelligible, but the scene with Timothy vivid, swift, convincing—a direct impression from the ugly, immediate fact.

He listened, his face lying on his arms. It was true, all true. She might have taken more and Timothy less; no doubt she was making it out as bad as she could for Timothy. But it lay between them—his wife and his son—it lay between them.

"An' I 'eard yer coming," she ended; "an' I thought I'd tell yer—an' I wor frightened about the 'arf-crowns—people 'ad been talkin' so at Dawson's—an' I didn't see no way out—an'—an'——"

She ceased, her hand plucking again at the comforter, her throat working.

He, too, thought of the loving words he had said to her, and the memory of them only made his misery the more fierce.

"An' there ain't no way out," he said violently, raising his head. "Yer'll be took before the magistrates next week, an' the assizes 'ull be in February, an' yer'll get six months—if yer don't get more."

She got up from her chair as though physically goaded by the words.

"I'll not go to jail," she said under her breath. "I'll not——"

A sound of scorn broke from Isaac.

"Yo' should ha' thought o' that," he said. "Yo' should ha' thought o' that. An' what you've been sayin' about Timothy don't make it a 'aporth the better—not for *yo'*! Yo' led *'im* into it too—if it 'adn't been for yo', 'ee'd never ha' *seen* the cursed stuff. Yo've dragged 'im down worse nor 'ee were—an' yerself—an' the childer—an' me. An' the drink, an' the lyin'!—it turns a man's stomach to think on it. An' I've been livin' with yer—these twelve years. I wish to the Lord I'd never seen yer—as the children 'ad never been born! They'll be known all their life now—as 'avin' 'ad sich a woman for their mother!"

A demon of passion possessed him more and more. He looked at her with murderous eyes, his hand on the table working.

For his world, too, lay in ruins about him. Through many hard-working and virtuous years he had counted among the righteous men of the village—the men whom the Almighty must needs reckon to the good whenever the score of Clinton Magna had to be made up. And this pre-eminence had come to be part of the habitual furniture of life and thought. To be suddenly stripped of it—to be not only disgraced by his wife, to be thrust down himself among the low and sinful herd—this thought made another man of him; made him wicked, as it were, perforce. For who that heard the story would ever believe that he was not the partner of her crime? Had he not eaten and drunk of it; were not he and his children now clothed by it?

Bessie did not answer him or look at him. At any other moment she would have been afraid of him; now she feared nothing but the image in her own mind—herself led along the village street, enclosed in that hateful building, cut off from all pleasure, all free moving and willing—alone and despised—her children taken from her.

Suddenly she walked into the back kitchen and opened the door leading to the garden.

Outside everything lay swathed in white, and a snowstorm was drifting over the deep cup of land which held the village. A dull, melancholy moonlight seemed to be somewhere behind the snow curtain, for the muffled shapes of the houses below and the long sweep of the hill were visible through the dark, and the objects in the little garden itself were almost distinct. There, in the centre, rose the round, stone edging of the well, the copious well, sunk deep into the chalk, for which Bessie's neighbours envied her, whence her good nature let them draw freely at any time of drought. On either side of it the gnarled stems of old fruit-trees and the bare sticks of winter kail made black scratches and blots upon the white.

Bessie looked out, leaning against the doorway, and heedless of the wind that drove upon her. Down below there was a light in Watson's cottage, and a few lights from the main street beyond pierced the darkness. The Spotted Deer must be at that moment full of people, all talking of her and Isaac. Her eye came hastily back to the snow-shrouded well and dwelt upon it.

"Shut that door!" Isaac commanded from inside. She obeyed, and came back into the kitchen. There she moved restlessly about a minute or two, followed by his frowning look—the look, not of a husband, but of an enemy. Then a sudden animal yearning for rest and warmth seized her. She opened the door by the hearth abruptly and went up, longing simply to lie down and cover herself from the cold.

But, after all, she turned aside to the children, and sat there for some time at the foot of the little boys' bed. The children, especially Arthur, had been restless for long, kept awake and trembling by the strange sounds outside their door and the loud voices downstairs; but, with the deep silence that had suddenly fallen on the house after Isaac had gone away to seek his interview with Watson, sleep had come to them, and even Arthur, on whose thin cheeks the smears left by crying were still visible, was quite unconscious of his mother. She looked at them from time to time, by the light of a bit of a candle she had placed on a box beside her; but she did not kiss them, and her eyes had no tears. From time to time she looked quickly round her, as though startled by a sound, a breathing.

Presently, shivering with cold, she went into her own room. There, mechanically, she took off her outer dress, as though to go to bed; but when she had done so her hands fell by her side; she stood motionless till, suddenly, wrapping an old shawl round her, she took up her candle and went downstairs again.

As she pushed open the door at the foot of the stairs she saw Isaac, where she had left him, sitting on his chair bent forward, his hands dropping between his knees, his gaze fixed on a bit of dying fire in the grate.

"Isaac!"

He looked up with the unwillingness of one who hates the sound he hears, and saw her standing on the lowest step. Her black hair had fallen upon her shoulders, her quick breath shook the shawl she held about her, and the light in her hand showed the anguished brightness of the eyes.

"Isaac, are yer comin' up?"

The question maddened him. He turned to look at her more fixedly.

"Comin' up? Noa, I'm not comin' up—so now know. Take yerself off, an' be quick."

She trembled.

"Are yer goin' to sleep down 'ere, Isaac?"

"Aye, or wherever I likes: it's no concern o' yourn. I'm no 'usband o' yourn from this day forth. Take yerself off, I say!—I'll 'ave no thief for *my* wife!"

But, instead of going, she stepped down into the kitchen. His words had broken her down; she was crying again.

"Isaac, I'd ha' put it back," she said, imploring. "I wor goin' in to Bedford to see Mr. Grimstone—'ee'd ha' managed it for me. I'd a' worked extra—I could ha' done it—if it 'adn't been for Timothy. If you'll 'elp—an' you'd oughter, for yer *are* my 'usband, whativer yer may say—we could pay John back—some day. Yo' can go to 'im, an' to Watson, an' say as we'll pay it back—yo' *could*, Isaac. I can take ter the plattin' again, an' I can go an' work for Mrs. Drew—she asked me again lasst week. Mary Anne 'ull see to the childer. Yo' go to John, Isaac, to-morrer—an'—an'—to Watson. All they wants is the money back. Yer couldn't—yer couldn't—see me took to prison, Isaac."

She gasped for breath, wiping the mist from her eyes with the edge of her shawl.

But all that she said only maddened the man's harsh and pessimist nature the more. The futility of her proposals, of her daring to think, after his fiat and the law's had gone forth, that there was any way out of what she had done, for her or for him, drove him to frenzy. And his wretched son was far away; so he must vent the frenzy on her. The melancholia, which religion had more or less restrained and comforted during a troubled lifetime, became, on this tragic night, a wild-beast impulse that must have its prey.

He rose suddenly and came towards her, his eyes glaring, and a burst of invective on his white lips. Then he made a rush for a heavy stick that leant against the wall.

She fled from him, reached her bedroom in safety, and bolted the door. She heard him give a groan on the stairs, throw away the stick and descend again.

Then, for nearly two hours, there was absolute stillness once more in this miserable house. Bessie had sunk, half fainting, on a chair by the bed, and lay there, her head lying against the pillow.

But in a very short time the blessed numbness was gone, and consciousness became once more a torture, the medium of terrors not to be borne. Isaac hated her—she would be taken from her children—she felt Watson's grip upon her arm—she saw the jeering faces at the village doors.

At times a wave of sheer bewilderment swept across her. How had it come about that she was sitting there like this? Only two days before she had been everybody's friend. Life had been perpetually gay and exciting. She had had qualms indeed, moments of a quick anguish, before the scene in the Spotted Deer. But there had been always some thought to protect her from herself. John was not coming back for a long, long time. She would replace the money—of course she would! And she would not take any more—or only a very little. Meanwhile, the hours floated by, dressed in a colour and variety they had never yet possessed for her—charged with all the delights of wealth, as such a human being under such conditions is able to conceive them.

Her nature, indeed, had never gauged its own capacities for pleasure till within the last few months. Excitement, amusement, society—she had grown to them; they had evoked in her a richer and fuller life, expanded and quickened all the currents of her blood. As she sat shivering in the darkness and solitude, she thought, with a sick longing, of the hours in the public-house—the lights, the talk, the warmth within and without. The drink-thirst was upon her at this moment. It had driven her down to the village that afternoon at the moment of John's arrival. But she had no money. She had not dared to unlock the cupboard again, and she could only wander up and down the bit of dark road beyond the Spotted Deer, suffering and craving. Well, it was all done—all done!

She had come up without her candle, and the only light in the room was a cold glimmer from the snow outside. But she must find a light, for she must write a letter. By much groping, she found some matches, and then lit one after another while she searched in her untidy drawers for an ink-bottle and a pen she knew must be there.

She found them, and with infinite difficulty—holding match after match in her left hand—she scrawled a few blotted lines on a torn piece of paper. She was a poor scholar, and the toil was great. When it was done, she propped the paper up against the looking-glass.

Then she felt for her dress, and deliberately put it on again, in the dark, though her hands were so numb with cold that she could scarcely hook the fastenings. Her teeth chattered as she threw her old shawl round her.

Stooping down, she took off her boots, and, pushing the bolt of her own door back as noiselessly as possible, she crept down the stairs. As she neared the lower door, the sound of two or three loud breathings caught her ear.

Her heart contracted with an awful sense of loneliness. Her husband slept—her children slept—while she——

Then the wave of a strange, a just passion mounted within her. She stepped into the kitchen, and, walking up to her husband's chair, she stood still a moment looking at him. The lamp was dying away, but she could still see him plainly. She held herself steadily erect; a frown was on her brow, a flame in her eyes.

"Well, good-bye, Isaac," she said, in a low but firm voice.

Then she walked to the back door and opened it, taking no heed of noise; the latch fell heavily, the hinges creaked.

"Isaac!" she cried, her tones loud and ringing, "*Isaac!*"

There was a sudden sound in the kitchen. She slipped through the door, and ran along the snow-covered garden.

Isaac, roused by her call from the deep trance of exhaustion which only a few minutes before had fallen upon his misery, stood up, felt the blast rushing in through the open door at the back, and ran blindly.

The door had swung to again. He clutched it open; in the dim, weird light he saw a dark figure stoop over the well; he heard something flung aside, which fell upon the snow with a thud; then the figure sprang upon the coping of the well.

He ran with all his speed, his face beaten by the wind and sleet. But he was too late. A sharp cry pierced the night. As he reached the well, and hung over it, he heard, or thought he heard, a groan, a beating of the water—then no more.

Isaac's shouts for help attracted the notice of a neighbour who was sitting up with her daughter and a new-born child. She roused her son-in-law and his boy, and, through them, a score of others, deep night though it was.

Watson was among the first of those who gathered round the well. He and others lowered Isaac with ropes into its icy depths, and drew him up again, while the snow beat upon them all—the straining men—the two dripping shapes emerging from the earth. A murmur of horror greeted the first sight of that marred face on Isaac's arm, as the lanterns fell upon it. For there was a gash above the eye, caused by a projection in the hard chalk side of the well, which of itself spoke death.

Isaac carried her in, and laid her down before the still glowing hearth. A shudder ran through him as he knelt, bending over her. The new wound had effaced all the traces of Timothy's blow. How long was it since she had stood there before him pointing to it? The features were already rigid. No one felt the smallest hope. Yet, with that futile tenderness all can show to the dead, everything was tried. Mary Anne Waller came—white and speechless—and her deft, gentle hands did whatever the village doctor told her. And there were many other women, too, who did their best. Some of them, had Bessie dared to live, would have helped with all their might to fill her cup of punishment to the brim. Now that she had thrown herself on death as her only friend, they were dissolved in pity.

Everything failed. Bessie had meant to die, and she had not missed her aim. There came a moment when the doctor, laying his ear for the last time to her cold breast, raised himself to bid the useless effort cease.

"Send them all away," he said to the little widow, "and you stay."

Watson helped to clear the room, then he and Isaac carried the dead woman upstairs. An old man followed them, a bent and broken being, who dragged himself up the steps with his stick; Watson out of compassion came back to help him.

"John—yer'd better go home, an' to yer bed—yer can't do no good."

"I'll wait for Mary Anne," said John, in a shaking whisper—"I'll wait for Mary Anne."

And he stood at the doorway, leaning on his stick; his weak and reddened eyes fixed on his cousin, his mouth open feebly.

But Mary Anne, weeping, beckoned to another woman who had come up with the little procession, and they began their last offices.

"Let us go," said the doctor kindly, his hand on Isaac's shoulder, "till they have done."

At that moment Watson, throwing a last professional glance round the room, perceived the piece of torn paper propped against the glass. Ah! there was the letter. There was always a letter.

He walked forward, glanced at it, and handed it to Isaac. Isaac drew his hand across his brow in bewilderment, then seemed to recognise the handwriting, and thrust it into his pocket without a word. Watson touched his arm. "Don't you destroy it," he said in warning; "it'll be asked for at the inquest."

The men descended. Watson and the doctor departed. John and Isaac were left alone in the kitchen. Isaac hung over the fire, which had been piled up in the hope of restoring warmth to the drowned woman. Suddenly he took out the letter and, bending his head to the blaze, began to read it.

"Isaac, yer a cruel husband to me, an' there's no way fer me but the way I'm goin'. I didn't mean no 'arm, not at first, but there, wot's the good of talkin'? I can't bear the way as you speaks to me an' looks at me, an' I'll never go to prison—no, never. It's orful—fer the children ull 'ave no mother, an' I don't know however Arthur 'ull manage. But yer woodent shew me no mercy, an' I can't think of anythin' different. I did love yer an' the childer, but the drink got holt of me. Yer mus' see as Arthur is rapped up, an' Edie's eyes 'ull 'ave to be seen to now an' agen. I'm sorry, but there's nothin' else. I wud like yer to kiss me onst, when they bring me in, and jes say, Bessie, I forgive yer. It won't do yer no 'arm, an' p'raps I may 'ear it without your knowin'. So good-bye, Isaac, from yur lovin' wife, Bessie. . . ."

As he read it, the man's fixed pallor and iron calm gave way. He leant against the mantelpiece, shaken at last with the sobs of a human and a helpless remorse.

John, from his seat on the settle a few yards away, looked at Isaac miserably. His lips opened now and then as though to speak, then closed again. His brain could form no distinct image. He was encompassed by a general sense of desolation, springing from the loss of his money, which was pierced every now and then by a strange sense of guilt. It seemed to have something to do with Bessie, this last, though what he could not have told.

So they sat, till Mary Anne's voice called "Isaac" from the top of the stairs.

Isaac stood up, drew one deep breath, controlled himself, and went, John following.

Mary Anne held the bedroom door open for them, and the two men entered, treading softly.

The women stood on either hand crying. They had clothed the dead in white and crossed her hands upon her breast. A linen covering had been passed, nun-like, round the head and chin. The wound was hidden and the face lay framed in an oval of pure white, which gave it a strange severity.

Isaac bent over her. Was this *Bessie*—Bessie, the human, faulty, chattering creature—whom he, her natural master, had been free to scold or caress at will? At bottom he had always been conscious in regard to her of a silent but immeasurable superiority, whether as a mere man to mere woman, or as the Christian to the sinner.

Now—he dared scarcely touch her. As she lay in this new-found dignity, the proud peace of her look intimidated, accused him—would always accuse him till he too rested as she rested now, clad for the end. Yet she had bade him kiss her—and he obeyed her—groaning within himself, incapable altogether, out of sheer abasement, of saying those words she had asked of him.

Then he sat down beside her, motionless. John tried once or twice to speak to him, but Isaac shook his head impatiently. At last the mere presence of Bolderfield in the room seemed to anger him. He threw the old man such dark and restless looks that Mary Anne perceived them, and, with instinctive understanding, persuaded John to go.

She, however, must needs go with him, and she went. The other woman stayed. Every now and then she looked furtively at Isaac.

"If some one don't look arter 'im," she said to herself, "'ee'll go as his father and his brothers went afore him. 'Ee's got the look on it awready. Wheniver it's light I'll go fetch Muster Drew."

With the first rays of the morning Bolderfield got up from the bed in Mary Anne's cottage, where she had placed him a couple of hours before, imploring him to lie still and rest himself. He slipped on his coat, the only garment he had taken off, and, taking his stick, he crept down to the cottage door. Mary Anne, who had gone out to fetch some bread, had left it ajar. He opened it and stood on the threshold, looking out.

The storm of the night was over, and already a milder breeze was beginning to melt the newly-fallen snow. The sun was striking cheerfully from the hill behind him upon the glistening surfaces of the distant fields; the old labourer felt a hint of spring in the air. It brought with it a hundred vague associations, and filled him with a boundless despair. What would become of him now—penniless and old and feeble? The horror of Bessie's death no longer stood between him and his own pain, and would soon even cease to protect her from his hatred.

Mary Anne came back along the lane, carrying a jug and a loaf. Her little face was all blanched and drawn with weariness, yet, when she saw him, her look kindled. She ran up to him.

"What did yer come down for, John? I'd ha' taken yer yer breakfast in yer bed."

He looked at her, then at the food. His eyes filled with tears.

"I can't pay yer for it," he said, pointing with his stick. "I can't pay yer for it."

Mary Anne led him in, scolding and coaxing him with her gentle, trembling voice. She made him sit down while she blew up the fire; she fed and tended him. When she had forced him to eat something, she came behind him and laid her hand on his shoulder.

"John," she said, clearing her throat. "John, yer shan't want while I'm livin'. I promised Eliza I wouldn't forget yer, and I won't. I can work yet—there's plenty o' people want me to work for 'em—an' maybe, when yer get over this, you'll work a bit too now and again. We'll hold together, John—anyways. While I live and keep my 'elth yer shan't want. An' yer'll forgive Bessie"—she broke into sudden sobbing. "Oh! I'll never 'ear a crule word about Bessie in my 'ouse, *never!*"

John put his arms on the table and hid his face upon them. He could not speak of forgiveness, nor could he thank her for her promise. His chief feeling was an intense wish to sleep; but, as Mary Anne dried her tears and began to go about her household work, the sound of her step, the sense of her loving presence near him, began, for the first time, to relax the aching grip upon his heart. He had always been weak and dependent, in spite of his thrift and his money. He would be far more weak and dependent now and henceforward. But again, he had found a woman's tenderness to lean upon, and, as she ministered to him—this humble, shrinking creature he had once so cordially despised—the first drop of balm fell upon his sore.

Meanwhile, in another cottage a few yards away, Mr. Drew was wrestling with Isaac. In his own opinion, he met with small success. The man who had refused his wife mercy shrank, with a kind of horror, from talking of the Divine mercy. Isaac Costrell's was a strange and groping soul. But those misjudged him who called him a hypocrite.

Yet in truth, during the years that followed, whenever he was not under the influence of recurrent attacks of melancholia, Isaac did again derive much comfort from the aspirations and self-abasements of religion. No human life would be possible if there were not forces in and round man perpetually tending to repair the wounds and breaches that he himself makes. Misery provokes pity; despair throws itself on a Divine tenderness. And for those who have the "grace" of faith, in the broken and imperfect action of these healing powers upon this various world—in the love of the merciful for the unhappy, in the tremulous, yet undying, hope that pierces even sin and remorse with the vision of some ultimate salvation from the self that breeds them — in these powers there speaks the only voice which can make us patient under the tragedies of human fate, whether these tragedies be "the falls of princes" or such meaner, narrower pains as brought poor Bessie Costrell to her end.

THE END.

Lector House believes that a society develops through a two-fold approach of continuous learning and adaptation, which is derived from the study of classic literary works spread across the historic timeline of literature records. Therefore, we aim at reviving, repairing and redeveloping all those inaccessible or damaged but historically as well as culturally important literature across subjects so that the future generations may have an opportunity to study and learn from past works to embark upon a journey of creating a better future.

This book is a result of an effort made by Lector House towards making a contribution to the preservation and repair of original ancient works which might hold historical significance to the approach of continuous learning across subjects.

HAPPY READING & LEARNING!

LECTOR HOUSE LLP
E-MAIL: lectorpublishing@gmail.com